"I have to be honest and up front about this pregnancy, Trent. You need to understand that I will never, ever give up my baby. I want you to give me sole custody."

While he'd known that was what Rebecca was after, it made him almost angry to hear her say it. "Am I such a bad guy?"

Her gaze dropped. "You're not a bad guy, no." Color stained her cheeks and she pressed her lips together.

It made him think of the kiss they'd shared earlier. That surprising burst of heat. Maybe he would be better off distancing himself permanently from her. From the baby.

But he couldn't! Memories slammed into him from all sides. Chubby cheeks, little fingers, hero worship. He couldn't lose another child. He couldn't.

"I have to be honest, too," he said. "I can't just walk away, Rebecca. Besides, our baby should have a mother and a father in its life. Full-time."

Rebecca shrugged. "That's ideal, but not a necessity."

"Well, maybe we should get married."

CHRISTIE RIDGWAY

A native Californian, Christie started reading and writing romances in middle school. It wasn't until she was the wife of her college sweetheart and the mother of two small sons that she submitted her work for publication. Many contemporary romances later, she is happiest when telling her stories despite the splash of kids in the pool, the mass of cups and plates in the kitchen and the many commitments she makes in the world beyond her desk.

Besides loving the men in her life and her dream-come-true job, she continues her longtime love affair with reading and is never without a stack of books. You can find out more about Christie at her Web site, www.christieridgway.com.

USA TODAY Bestselling Author

CHRISTIE RIDGWAY
RIGHT BY HER SIDE

Published by Silhouette Books
America's Publisher of Contemporary Romance

Special thanks and acknowledgment are given to
Christie Ridgway for her contribution
to the LOGAN'S LEGACY series.

SILHOUETTE BOOKS

Recycling programs
for this product may
not exist in your area.

ISBN-13: 978-0-373-36357-5

RIGHT BY HER SIDE

Be a part of

*Because birthright has its privileges
and family ties run deep.*

**She is pregnant with his baby, and when he
learns of his impending fatherhood,
he proposes a marriage of convenience.
Will love enter the bargain?**

Trent Crosby: He conducted his personal life as
he would a business meeting. So when he heard
Rebecca's news, he made her an offer she couldn't
refuse…until she did. Suddenly he had to raise
the stakes and risk everything!

Rebecca Holley: She wanted her baby to have
it all, so when Trent proposed a marriage of
convenience, she was definitely tempted.
He was charming and a good provider, but did he
feel the same stirring of attraction that she felt?
And did this have the potential to be more than
just a business arrangement?

Baby recovered! After a frantic search,
Lisa Sanders's adorable baby was recovered
unharmed and in good health. The tight
community of Portland rejoiced! But one more
mystery was still unsolved….

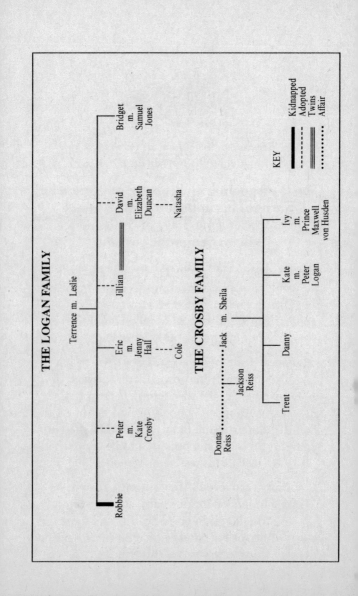

THE LOGAN FAMILY

Terrence m. Leslie

Robbie

Peter
m.
Kate Crosby

Eric
m.
Jenny Hall

Jillian

David
m.
Elizabeth Duncan

Bridget
m.
Samuel Jones

Cole

Natasha

THE CROSBY FAMILY

Donna Reiss

Jack m. Sheila

Jackson Reiss

Trent

Danny

Kate
m.
Peter Logan

Ivy
m.
Prince Maxwell von Husden

KEY

Kidnapped
Adopted
Twins
Affair

*Because birthright has its privileges
and family ties run deep.*

Prologue

The man across the heavy, gleaming desk cleared his throat. "Rebecca, I know who fathered your child."

Rebecca Holley blinked. When she'd been called away from her shift as an OR pediatric nurse to meet with Morgan Davis at the Children's Connection facility adjacent to Portland General, she hadn't known what to expect. Certainly not a statement of the obvious.

"Well, of course you know, Morgan." Though the sperm donor had been anonymous to her, as director of the fertility clinic where she'd been inseminated, the man sitting opposite her had access to the complete records. Her palm slid across the lavender smock of her Minnie Mouse-printed scrubs to rest over her still-flat stomach. At seven weeks pregnant she'd yet to experience morning sickness, but the odd expression on Morgan's face was beginning to make her queasy.

She cleared her throat. "What's going on?"

"Rebecca…" His gaze dropped to the open folder on his desk and then moved back up to meet her eyes. "There's no easy way to say this."

Now her stomach mimicked a dying fish—flop, flop, flop. "The pregnancy test wasn't wrong, was it?"

"No, no! You're pregnant." Leaning forward, he lowered his voice. "But we recently discovered a mix-up of some donor vials, so we went back and checked our recent insemination cases."

A mix-up? Rebecca swallowed, trying to stay calm. He was telling her there had been a mix-up of donor sperm. As a nurse, she could see why the clinic would be concerned about an error, but how could such a thing affect her? She'd looked over the profiles of the donors and selected one with a working-class background— he'd spent time as an enlisted navy man like her dad— who was dark-haired and dark-eyed like herself.

But she wasn't picky.

She let out a little laugh to cover her nervousness. "As long as the baby's healthy, Morgan, it won't matter to me—even if it's as blond-haired as…Blondie."

Morgan glanced down at the folder again and grimaced. "Your baby may very well look as you describe, Rebecca. We inseminated you with the sperm of a blond-haired man. A very wealthy, respected man…and one who didn't provide his sperm for this purpose."

"But that doesn't matter, right?" Rebecca pressed her palm against her stomach. *Don't worry, Eisenhower.* The nickname tumbled into her mind, and she almost smiled at the old family joke. It was the name Rebecca's folks had used when referring to each of her four younger brothers and sisters before they were born. Apparently she was going to carry on the tradition.

Eisenhower, it's going to be okay.

"Everything's still anonymous, Morgan," Rebecca continued. "*I* don't know the man. I don't know who the father is."

Morgan shook his head. "But this man has a right to know he *is* going to be a father, Rebecca. Children's Connection can't keep this a secret from him."

She found herself rising to her feet, her voice rising, too. "What? Why not?" Her protective instincts were quivering like antennae, though it was hard to wrap her mind around all the ramifications this "mix-up" might mean to her and her baby.

"It's the ethical thing to do, Rebecca. You can see that."

What she could see was her hopes and her dreams turning from something joyful to something dreadful. No, no! She couldn't think like that. She wouldn't. Her baby was still *her* baby. "Who is this man, Morgan? You let me talk to him and I'll…I'll straighten it out." She'd explain what had happened and then assure him that she and Eisenhower expected nothing from him whatsoever.

Morgan frowned. "Rebecca—"

"You owe me, too, Morgan," she said, her voice

sounding thin and breathless. "You owe me the chance to talk to this man first."

His frown deepened. "Rebecca—"

"Tell me who he is, Morgan."

Morgan and his wife were in the process of adopting a baby and it must have given him sympathy for Rebecca's fierce desperation because he glanced down at the file once more, then sighed. "The father of your baby is Trent Crosby, Rebecca. Trent Crosby, the Crosby Systems CEO."

One

It was past six o'clock when Rebecca steered her hatchback into a spot in the far corner of the Crosby Systems near-empty parking lot and turned off the ignition. Her fingers unclipped her Portland General Hospital name badge from her scrubs to stuff it into the purse on the passenger seat beside her.

Then she looked up at the rearview mirror, gazing at the reflection of the Crosby building's gleaming glass front doors. "Okay, Eisenhower," she said in a brisk voice. "It's time for us to get this over with."

Rebecca discovered that her legs didn't share her can-do attitude, however, and that her behind was determined to remain glued to the vinyl driver's seat. When she tried again to leave her car, again nothing happened.

"Eisenhower," Rebecca muttered, "your mom's no wimp. Honest." But she was acting like one. She snuck another glance at the rearview mirror. It was the Crosby name that was spooking her. She knew about the family: they were powerful and they were rich. It didn't help that she'd caught a glimpse of Trent himself at a charity auction last December, because beyond being powerful and rich he had something else intimidating going for him, too.

"You're getting some seriously good-looking genes, Eisenhower," she whispered. "No doubt about it."

Maybe she shouldn't have insisted on breaking the news herself, she thought. Maybe she should let Morgan tell him, man-to-man, and then she could wait for Mr. Rich, Powerful and Good-Looking to approach *her.*

But no! The last thing she wanted was to be at the emotional mercy of some man, right? Been there, done that, got the painful divorce.

So she forced her feet from the car, slammed shut the door, then reminded herself of the number of new situations she'd faced as a navy brat. Those eight moves in seventeen years had made her an expert at assessing new people and new surroundings and then finding a way to fit in—or at least fade into the woodwork. It was why she'd insisted on talking to Trent herself. She was practiced in making herself appear agreeable and non-threatening, certainly a big plus at a moment like this.

So there was absolutely no reason to hesitate. Squaring her shoulders, she faced the company entrance and…

…let her gaze wander to the freshly painted Dumpsters off to her right. She told herself she wasn't putting off the inevitable. She told herself it was because her attention was snagged by several appliance-size, empty cardboard boxes sitting beside them. Boxes of the ideal size and condition for that playhouse she'd been promising to make for her favorite pediatric patient.

Rebecca glanced up at the cloud-filled sky. It had rained that morning and now it looked as if it might rain again. She could take the few moments necessary to flatten the boxes and stow them safely away in her car.

It wasn't stalling!

It wasn't as simple as it should have been, either. First, her slick-soled white nurse's shoes slid on a patch of squishy mud in the Dumpster area, sending her down on one knee and sprouting a dirty stain on her pants leg. Second, the boxes had stubborn, reinforced corners that resisted her efforts to collapse them. Third, when she indulged in a foot-stamp of frustration, she sent a spray of mud droplets into the air, to land who knew where.

Fourth, when she crawled beneath the open end of the largest box to see if she could find a way to flatten the thing from the inside, she heard a man's voice float through the air. "Can I help you?"

She froze. Whoever belonged to that deep voice, perhaps he wasn't talking to her. Perhaps he was talking to someone else in the lot, someone having an innocuous, employee-going-home problem such as too much to carry or a recalcitrant car door lock. Some run-of-the-mill, easy-to-resolve problem.

Happening to someone else. *Please.*

"You there in the box," the man spoke again, squashing her hopes. "Can I help you?"

Rebecca cleared her throat. "Are you, um, talking to me?"

"Believe it or not, you're the only one wearing cardboard in my entire parking lot." There wasn't a whiff of humor in the voice.

His parking lot? Was this Trent Crosby? This was as bad as it could be.

In the evening light coming through the open top flaps above her head, Rebecca glanced at the muddy knee of her scrubs, then the fine sprinkling of drying dirt on her forearms, then the corrugated camouflage surrounding her. *Oh, Eisenhower, this isn't the meeting I planned for us.*

"I was just, uh, driving by and spotted the boxes," she said.

"Just driving by, huh?"

She swallowed her groan. The company was located at the farthest corner of a business and industrial complex that could only be reached by a dead-end parkway. It was impossible to "drive by" the place. Instead of answering, she edged toward her car—she hoped she was heading in that direction, anyway—taking her disguise along with her. The scurrying box had to look ridiculous to him, she knew that, but not half as ridiculous as she would feel if she had to introduce herself to Mr. Rich, Powerful and Good-Looking when she was dirty, disheveled and not yet ready to meet him.

Her box bumped into something. She halted, uncertain of what that something might be.

"Come on, now. Exactly what are you doing in our garbage?"

The close proximity of the voice made it clear she'd bumped into *him*. She chanced a peek upward. The giant-size box was taller than the man, so she couldn't see his face and he couldn't see hers.

"Stop playing games, damn it. What the hell are you doing with our garbage?"

But she didn't need to see him to understand he was more than suspicious. "It's not garbage," she replied, hoping to placate him. "It's a box." Moving like a hermit crab, she set off in the general direction of her car once more. "For a playhouse."

There was a moment of silence.

She bumped into something again.

Him. He'd moved to block her way, she realized, as the box was whisked over her head, leaving her blinking in the now-brighter light. Though she resisted the urge to cover herself, she had to look up—it was instinctive—and then she jumped back and looked away. That was instinctive, too. Like the sun, blond-haired, brown-eyed Trent Crosby was dazzling.

There was no chance she was carrying his child, she decided, his lean features and rangy body already forever etched in her mind. He had a confident, very male brand of beauty that oozed power and wealth. He couldn't be the father of her baby, absolutely not, because such a thing went against the laws of the universe.

They were from two different worlds. The last time she'd tried bridging such a gap, she'd found herself taking a shortcut to humiliation and heartache.

"A playhouse, you say." He repeated her words in a flat, cool voice.

Rebecca could only nod, hyperconscious of everything that was wrong with her, from her muddy scrubs to the way her brown hair frizzed when there was rain in the air. She reached up both palms to slick back the inevitable, messy tendrils that were surely springing at her temples, smoothing them toward the efficient twist she wore during work hours.

"You'll have to come up with something better than that. You get a playhouse at a toy store, not a Dumpster, sweetheart. I can guess what you're really after."

Her head jerked up. "Huh?"

In a light charcoal suit, white shirt and true-blue tie, Trent Crosby was staring down at her through narrowed eyes. "Our history—both past and very recent—has made us careful, honey. And ruthless. You won't find our company secrets in these garbage bins, but regardless, we prosecute wanna-be corporate spies, even little cuddly ones like you."

"*What?*"

He smiled at her, a cold display of perfect white teeth that sent shivers running for cover down her back. "And if you're not off my property in thirty seconds, I'll be happy to haul you into the security office for an after-hours strip search."

She didn't need ten seconds to be back in her car and

accelerating out of the parking lot. A glance in her rear-view mirror confirmed what she could feel in the second flurry of shivers rolling down her spine. He was watching her leave, his crossed arms shouting out his satisfaction.

"Believe me, Eisenhower," she whispered. "He can't be your daddy." Because the heat of humiliation on her cheeks told her Trent Crosby was from a different world, all right. The Planet of the Jerks.

At 4:00 p.m. the next day, Trent Crosby departed the executive conference room of Crosby Systems, his mind teeming with the details of the new contract he'd sewn up that afternoon. He decided to draft a memo on it to the Research and Development Department before leaving for the day. Between the memo and the reports stacked up on his desk for review, he'd be in his chair well past midnight. The thought made him almost cheerful.

He was more comfortable at Crosby Systems than in the morgue he called home.

Half a hall-length from his office, his assistant way-laid him, snatching the coffee mug out of his hand and tsking. "Nuh-uh-uh. Remember how even bossier and more bad-tempered we get on too much caffeine? We can't have another five-pot day."

Ah. An impending skirmish with the battle-ax who ruled the top floor. Damn, Trent thought, things kept getting better. He drew in a deep, threatening breath and glowered down at her. "*We* aren't having a five-pot day. *I* am. You drink that disgusting green tea."

"I'm going to live forever on that green tea," Claudine retorted.

"Then I'm praying for my own early grave." He made a grab for his cup, but she whisked it behind her back. Strong-arming her was tempting, but Trent was wary of that determined glitter in her eye, even if she was on the upside of sixty.

Even after ten years of *her* working for *him*, she could still scare the hell out of him.

"I said no more coffee," Claudine declared again. "We don't want you polishing that nasty mean streak of yours on the pretty young woman who just arrived."

"Nasty mean streak? Don't blame that on the coffee, you old biddy. It comes from putting up with you." Then he frowned. "Wait a minute. What pretty young woman?"

"The one in your office. And don't ask me what she wants. She said her business is personal." Claudine reached up to straighten his tie.

He batted her hand away, wondering who had personal business with him. He, as a rule, didn't get personal with people.

His assistant stretched toward his tie again, and again he evaded her fussing. "Leave me be, you old bag. Which reminds me, aren't you past our mandatory retirement age yet?"

She snorted. "I'll be here, still cleaning up your messes when *you* retire. Now get into your office and find out why a nice woman would have personal dealings with a temperamental dictator like you."

He narrowed his eyes. "Harridan."

She mimicked his glare. "Tyrant."

"Fishwife."

"Martinet."

Then they smiled at each other and set off in opposite directions.

Trent was still smiling when he pushed open the door to his office. But the smile died as the "nice" and "pretty" woman in one of his visitors' chairs jumped to her feet and swung around to face him. It was the box lady.

"You," he said.

The first thing out of her mouth was something he already knew. "I'm *not* a corporate spy."

Of course she wasn't, he acknowledged, letting out an inward sigh. But he'd been grinding his teeth through a brutal headache yesterday when he'd glimpsed someone skulking around the Dumpsters and he'd flashed on the ugly explanation. Claudine accused him of cynicism.

The way he figured it, expecting the worst of people ensured he was never disappointed.

"I know you're not a spy," Trent admitted to the young woman. "As you were scuttling to your car, I realized you couldn't be."

She blinked. "What cleared it up for you?"

The little thing had big brown eyes, the long-lashed kind that made him think of Disney characters or his sisters' baby dolls. "The scrubs. Maybe if they were that sick, surgical green, but ones like yours…" He gestured, indicating the loose-fitting pants and smock that enveloped her. Today they were lemon-yellow and printed with cross-eyed clown fish. "Not spy wear."

She didn't respond, only continued standing there, staring at him with…anticipation? Expectation? Trent stared back, cursing Claudine for denying him his jolt of caffeine. He needed something to pop out the apology Big Brown Eyes obviously awaited.

"Look—"

"Look—"

They spoke the word at the same time and when she broke off, she flushed. It took his attention off those Bambi eyes and onto her fair, fine-pored complexion. For a second he wondered what her skin would feel like beneath his stroking thumb.

Damn, he needed that coffee.

"Look, I'm sorry, okay?" he said, shoving his hands in his pockets. "Is that what you're after?"

"No!" Her head shook back and forth. "I don't want anything from you. That's, uh, that's why I'm here."

Okay. Stumped by that puzzling remark, he watched her suck in her bottom lip, worry it a moment, then let it pop free. Inside his pockets, his fingers curled as he found himself with a sudden fascination for her mouth. Her little suck-worry-pop had flushed it rosier. The lips looked soft and pillowy.

He hadn't had a good nap in a long, long while.

Forcing himself to look away, he crossed to his desk and sat down. *Get your mind back on business, Trent.* Think of the memo. The reports. The satisfying hours of work ahead.

He didn't have the time or inclination for romance, and this woman, with her baby-fine skin and her wavy hair, had a face that resembled a sentimentalized Victorian valentine. The face alone shouted she wasn't his type, but then there were those figure-shrouding scrubs. Trent liked women who wore tight minis and flashy Manolos, women who liked their encounters as brief as their skirts and their men as blunt and to the point as their high heels.

This woman didn't come close to that description.

Determined to get her out of his office and get on with the rest of his workday, he focused on her Portland General Hospital name tag. "Well, Rebecca Holley, R.N., I'm a busy man. Why, exactly, did you stop by?"

She sank into the chair across from his desk, doing that distracting suck-worry-pop with her lower lip again. "This is a little difficult to say…."

But to his shock, she managed to get it out, anyway, in a few brief sentences. A mix-up at Children's Connection. His sperm. Her pregnancy. Throughout her explanation, Trent could only stare at her again, numb.

Disbelieving.

Disbelieving and numb.

When she wound down, he realized she expected a response from him. "My sisters put you up to this," he tried. "It's a little late for April Fools', but—"

"I wouldn't joke about something like this," she snapped, her spine straightening and her voice sharpening. "I wouldn't joke about my baby."

Baby. *Baby.*

Memories rushed into his mind. His sisters as chubby, chortling infants. The hero worship in his little brother's eyes. The hair rising on the back of his nine-year-old neck the day Robbie Logan had gone missing while playing at their house. Twenty-plus years later, the choking sensation in his lungs when he'd learned his baby nephew had been kidnapped.

Then that sickening, bat-to-the-gut blow when his wife had stood in an examining room at Children's Connection and finally admitted that the only fertility problem she suffered from was him. That she'd lied about going off the pill because she didn't want to bear his child—or even be married to him any longer.

Yesterday's headache slammed into the base of his skull and lingered there, pulsing pain. "It's a joke," he said aloud, his voice harsh. "It's got to be someone's idea of a joke."

His gaze lasered on the pretty little Victorian valentine who might not be a spy, but who was playing some criminal game all the same. He pointed his finger at her, but kept the volume of his voice under strict control. "And I won't be laughing if you're still sitting here when I get back."

With that, he rose to his feet and stalked toward the door. He pulled it open.

"Wait—"

But he didn't pay attention to the woman. Instead he marched unseeing into the hall, almost knocking his assistant over. His hands shot out and he steadied her. "Sorry, Claudine. I'm sorry."

She stared up at him. "Trent? What's the matter?"

Nothing. Everything. It *couldn't* be true. He swung

his head around, trying to find something else to focus on. Proposals. Reports. Spreadsheets. The business details that had always filled his life.

But he couldn't turn off thoughts of chortling babies, missing children, kidnapped toddlers. Hopes that had never been born.

Then he sensed movement behind him, and knew he couldn't stay a moment longer. He couldn't face *her,* the woman who'd dredged up all this in his mind. Already heading for the stairs, he called back to Claudine, "Take the rest of the afternoon off. You deserve it."

"No! The company bully is giving me time off? And going home early himself?"

He didn't have the heart to come up with a matching insult. But that was good, wasn't it?

After all, hearts were a damn inconvenience.

Two

After a long, less-than-uplifting day at the hospital, Rebecca was halfway up the walk to her small duplex when she halted, arrested by the sight of a pair of men's leather loafers resting on her welcome mat. She was still blinking at them when they moved, and the body they were attached to shifted from its position against her shadowed front door and into the evening light.

Trent Crosby. He'd strode out of his office the day before, his face expressionless, and she hadn't heard from him since. She'd dared to hope it would stay that way.

"What do you want?" she called out, not getting any closer to him. She had reason to be wary. He'd accused her of being a spy one day and a prankster the next. Who knew what would come out of the man's mouth now?

"We need to talk," he said, his voice quiet. His steady gaze met hers. "You need to give me a chance."

She'd already given him a chance. Yesterday. Though she'd been embarrassed by their encounter in the parking lot the day before *that*, by the time she'd driven home she'd rethought the situation. In good conscience she couldn't blame the confusion on him, not when she hadn't stuck around long enough to clear things up. So she'd tried again, with no better results.

As she continued to study him in silence, he took a step closer.

She took a step back.

He stilled. "I'll make it worth your while." His watchful expression eased into a coaxing smile. "I've brought you a present."

Oh, no. That charming smile scared the heck out of her, because it slid over his mouth with so little effort and then without any more it was already affecting her, warming her icy misgivings of him.

So she scowled. "Present?"

She reminded herself that rich men found it easy to hand out gifts. Her ex had been big on giving them, too. The ones he'd charged to their credit cards had tipped her off that he was cheating on her, because the glittering baubles and sexy little nothings hadn't come *her* way. "What kind of present?"

Trent half turned and dragged something over that she hadn't noticed in the shadows of her porch.

"Boxes," he said. "There was a pile by the Dumpsters as I was leaving the office today and I thought of you."

He'd brought her boxes.

Of course, the only reason why that knowledge was melting the ice inside her was because she'd spent an hour after her shift with Merry, the asthmatic child to whom she'd promised a playhouse. Those boxes meant she could tell the little girl tomorrow that she was making progress on the project.

With that in mind, she hurried toward Trent. He'd brought boxes all right. Six flattened boxes of the ideal, extra-large size that would provide the main construction materials for the kid-size cottage she had in mind. "Thank you," she said, thinking of Merry again. Rebecca's fingers tightened on her keys as she took a breath. "I suppose…I suppose you can come in."

But she'd keep her guard up. That wouldn't be hard. Her navy-brat years, while they had given her good skills in getting along with people, had also trained her to maintain a safe distance from them as well. Not only wasn't it smart to trust others on short acquaintance, but if you got too close, it hurt too much when the next base posting came along. And then there were the lessons her ex had taught her…

Trent followed her through the front door into her small living room. As she hung her purse on the bent-wood coatrack that stood beside the door, from the corner of her eye she saw him taking in the surroundings. A tissue-thin Oriental carpet over clean but scratched hardwood. A love seat "slipcovered" with an old quilt she'd found at a yard sale and then tucked around the torn cushions. The simple curtains that had started life as sheets until she and her sewing machine had spent some time with them. The cinder-block-and-plywood shelves that were the staple of college students and women who were restarting their lives after a failed marriage.

As she turned to face him, she felt herself bristling. He couldn't think much of her modest home.

His gaze moved from the entry that led to her never-remodeled kitchen and onto her face. "Nice," he said. "Homey."

Hah. Homely was more like it. But there wasn't a note of snideness to his voice or any derision in his eyes.

The crack in the ice inside her widened more. "Well, you might as well come into the kitchen," she said. It wasn't any fancier than the rest of the place. "Would you like some cold tea?"

He would, and she poured it as he took a seat at the tiny table. When she slid the glass in front of him, he stared into its depths.

"Green tea?"

"Yes, it's decaffeinated. Is that all right?"

He nodded without looking up. "It's perfect. Just perfect."

She pulled out the other chair and dropped into it. As her bottom settled onto the seat, the past few sleepless nights and her long shift at the hospital seemed to settle onto her shoulders. Lifting her own glass of tea, she tried to hide her sigh of fatigue.

But his hearing must be excellent. "Is something the matter?" he asked.

She tried to smile. "Nothing more than a long day, pregnancy and a strange man in my kitchen." Tiredness soaked into her bones.

His gaze sharpened on her. "Have you eaten?"

"Sometime today." Her hand waved. "Lunch."

He was out of his chair and rummaging through her cupboards before she could blink. "You need food."

"Wait, no—"

"Stay," he ordered, as she started to push her chair back. "I'm a bachelor. I can scrounge together the semblance of a meal when I have to."

Surprise kept her glued to her seat. In silence, she watched as he made up a plate of crackers accompanied by slices of cheese and apple.

Then he set it in front of her with a no-nonsense *clack*. "Now eat. Are you taking prenatal vitamins?"

Her jaw dropped. "Um, yes. How did you—"

"Sisters. Two of 'em. One a new mother, the other one pregnant." His head swung around and he swooped down on a plastic bottle near the sink, then placed it in front of her. "In the early days, the vitamins made Ivy queasy unless she ate them with crackers. For Katie, it was cold, buttered spaghetti."

"They don't bother me," Rebecca murmured. In spite of herself, she was…intrigued. Oh, fine. She was almost charmed. Who would have thought that this big bad businessman knew the details of his sisters' pregnancies? "You're, uh, well-educated."

He shrugged, then sat down and nudged the plate of food closer to her. "Well-informed is more like it. I'm the oldest in the family. I grew up wiping noses and doling out kiddie aspirin. I guess the younger ones still tell me when they don't feel well."

"I'm the oldest, too." But while her siblings had looked up to her as the big sister, they'd gone to Mom or Pop when they were sick.

Instead of responding to that, he reached over to slap a piece of cheese on a cracker, then he lifted her hand and dropped the cracker on the flat of her palm. "Eat," he commanded.

"All right, all right." Her first bite tasted heavenly, but then that fatigue turned into full-blown exhaustion. Each subsequent chew seemed to take more and more energy.

"I spoke with Morgan Davis," Trent said.

Rebecca swallowed, a shot of adrenaline making her more alert. "And?"

"And he explained there had indeed been a mix-up. They're trying to track down the exact problem. He told me he's concerned about the clinic's reputation and potential legal problems. But Children's Connection has done so much good that I've assured him I won't sue. He said you told him the same." Trent ran his hands through his hair. "So, I'm, uh, sorry about the way I reacted yesterday afternoon when you told me. I wasn't expecting…"

"That I was, and thanks to you?"

He blinked, then laughed. "Yes. Exactly."

Rebecca smiled back at him; she couldn't help herself. With the light of humor in his eyes, with that easy grin on his face, it was hard to think of him as the rich, powerful Trent Crosby who might threaten the happy future she'd planned for herself and Eisenhower.

He was just a man, a caring man, who had brought her boxes and knew something about pregnancy. It *was* going to be all right, she thought, and then said it out loud. "It's going to be all right."

Trent's gaze swept over her, then around the kitchen. "Yes, I agree. I think it's going to be fine."

Rebecca managed another sip of her tea, but her head felt so very, very heavy. Her pregnancy book said that tiredness in the first trimester was common, and she was tired. Very, very tired.

"Rebecca?"

At her name, her lashes lifted. Had she dozed off? Her face flushed. It wasn't like her to fall asleep at the table, not to mention in the company of a man she didn't know, a man she couldn't afford to trust so soon—if ever. "Yes?"

He was pulling her out of her chair. "Let me help you. You look beat."

Her feet must have been moving, because she was leaving the kitchen. Trent had his arm around her and she could smell the scent of him. It was spicy, good, and if she wasn't so very sleepy, she might like to bury her nose against the tan column of his throat.

"Let's get you to your bedroom, Rebecca."

Her feet stopped moving. *"What?"*

He chuckled. "Don't rouse yourself. I just want to help you to bed before you start snoring on your kitchen table."

"I don't snore," she protested. But he wanted to help her. That sounded nice. And she thought maybe she could trust him to do it, because he was an older brother and knew about prenatal vitamins. "This way to my bed." She managed to point with a limp finger, and then her hand fell.

He laughed again, then directed her down the short hallway to her small room. Rebecca didn't think about how shabby it must look in his eyes. She only thought about the bed and her pillow and how good she'd feel under the light weight of the last blanket her mother had ever crocheted.

In moments it was just as she imagined. Trent must have taken off her shoes—she knew she didn't have the energy for it—because her toes wiggled freely as he stood beside the bed, looking down at her.

"Good night, Rebecca Holley, R.N."

"Good night, Trent Crosby." *Big bad businessman— not.* "Sorry we didn't get to talk more."

But they would, because he was a nice man. A trust-worthy man who would stay out of her and her baby's life when she asked him to. Which she would. A yawn nearly cracked her jaw in two.

He lingered.

"Is there something you wanted to say?" she asked, the words slurring as her eyes drifted closed. "Sorry, but I worked a long shift and I'm so, so tired."

"I can see that. And I have a solution to our problem that I'd like you to think about."

"Mmmmm." She wasn't even sure he was still

nearby, or that she was still awake. Tomorrow she'd think about how she could relax with a stranger in her room. Oh, but that answer was easy, because he was trustworthy, after all. She knew that now.

So she let herself slide into slumber. His last words drifted into her ears and then drifted out before they could trigger a nightmare.

"Once you have the baby," Trent's voice said, "if you give custody to me, I'll give you half a million dollars."

Sitting at his desk, Trent doodled on a pad, then caught himself and threw down his pen in disgust. He didn't doodle!

He refocused his attention on the report opened in front of him. It wasn't any more interesting than it had been five minutes before, but he made himself read every damn word. Then he checked the time again.

Two-thirty. Forty-two hours. He hadn't seen or heard from Rebecca Holley in forty-two hours. Well-practiced in negotiation, he knew the next move was hers, but the waiting was driving him nuts. Admitting his concentration was shot, he pushed up from his chair and headed out of his office.

Claudine looked up from her desk, situated a few steps from his door. "Have we finished going over the departmental reports?"

He gave her his best malevolent glare, all the while blessing her for offering the distraction. "Again? How many times do I have to tell you not to refer to me as 'we'?"

"It's the royal 'we,'" she replied. "Because you're a royal pain in the patoot."

He would have laughed, but he didn't like giving her the satisfaction. Instead, he stalked past her.

"Where are you going, your majesty?" she called out.

"Human Resources. To get the necessary forms to have you fired."

"Without me, you couldn't *find* Human Resources, let alone fill out one of their forms."

"Shrew." He strode into the hall.

"Despot."

Still moving, he raised his voice, determined to get in the last word. "Nag."

Her response reached his ears, anyway. "Oligarch."

That one stopped him. He retraced his steps and poked his head into her sanctum. "Oligarch? That's good. That's very good."

Claudine's smile was smug. "Of course I am."

He snorted, then started to move off again.

"Trent?" Claudine again.

But this time her tone lacked its usual caustic edge, causing him to backtrack once more to meet her gaze. "Is something the matter?"

"That was my question." Her eyes were serious, her expression kind. "Is there a problem I can help you with? All of us in Admin talked over lunch and we realize something's bothering you. We'd...well, we'd like to help if we can."

Oh, hell. If Admin was talking about him... Next thing he knew, his competitors would get wind of his lack of focus and use it against the company. When he found himself distracted, then doodling, then drawing the concern of his domineering assistant and her henchmen, it was time to take a new tack in the negotiations.

He sighed. "Cover for me, will you, Claudine? I might be out a couple of hours."

It was time to confront Rebecca Holley and demand—in concise, clear terms—what he wanted from her.

Problem was, Trent thought a short car ride later, it was going to be hard to make any kind of demand to a woman sitting on the floor with a baby in her lap and a bigger kid hanging around her neck. Peering around a large poster announcing a children's health fair in the hospital parking lot the following weekend, he watched her through the glass door leading into the crowded playroom on the Pediatrics floor. After another minute, though, he pushed open the door and walked in, because she was laughing and…and the happy expression on her face made him feel as if he hadn't laughed since he was nine years old and Robbie Logan had gone missing while Trent was playing basketball in the rear yard.

She glanced up as he strode into the room, the smile on her face dying. "Oh!"

The last time he'd seen her, her face had been pale with fatigue and her eyes heavy with sleep, but now she looked flushed and alert. "Rebecca." He nodded a greeting.

She rose to her feet, cradling the baby in her arms. Trent noticed the little guy had two full leg casts and three teeth.

"Gawaa!" Three-Teeth said, waving a fat arm.

Rebecca's cheek touched the top of the baby's head, a caress so natural he wondered if she was even aware of it. "This is Vince, one of my pediatric OR patients," she said, then looked down at the other child she'd been playing with. "And Merry."

"Nice to meet you," Trent said, nodding again.

Merry wiggled the fingers of her thin hand.

Baby Vince made another wild gesture, a right hook that almost connected with Rebecca's nose. "Gawaa! *Gawaa!*"

"Right back at ya," Trent murmured, coming close enough to capture the contender's little fist. The baby grinned at him, then took Trent's hand to his mouth to gnaw on it like a bone.

"Oh, sorry." Rebecca tried to step back, but Trent halted her movement by capturing one of her shoulders in his other hand. Beneath his palm, the small curve felt feminine, delicate, reminding him of how fragile she'd seemed when he'd helped her to her bedroom.

"Have you been eating?" His voice sounded abrupt, he knew it, but thinking about her body beneath those dumpy scrubs was doing something to him…. Arousing him. Making him worried, because getting hot over a woman covered in pale pink with raspberry flamingos had to be the first symptom of some weird sexual perversion.

"I've been eating fine," Rebecca assured him. "And getting more rest, too." Her face flushed as bright as those long-legged birds she was wearing and she

glanced around at the kids and their parents who were
involved with toys or puzzles or who were watching
some kids' show on the TV in the corner of the room.
"I want you to know I'm sorry about dozing off on you
the other night. I've never done that before."

"It's all right."

"Well, thank you." Her forehead wrinkled. "Is
there…something you wanted?"

He frowned. He wanted her response to his proposition, of course. Then he jumped, startled by the sharp
nip Vince gave his knuckle. "Yowch!"

The little guy grinned without an ounce of repen-
tance. "Ga—"

"—waa. I know, kid. And a gawaa to you, too."

Rebecca tried shifting the baby away, but Vince
wasn't having it. With another "gawaa," he held his
arms out to Trent, smiling so widely that a big dollop
of drool oozed over his bottom lip.

In one smooth move, Trent pulled his handkerchief
from his pocket, dabbed off the kid's chin, and then
took him in his own arms.

Rebecca blinked, then looked down at Merry, who
looked back with the same surprise mirrored on her face.
"So much for the big, bad businessman, eh, Merry?"

The little girl hid her answering smile behind her hand.

"Huh?" Trent lifted a brow. "Big bad businessman?"

"Inside joke," Rebecca said, not meeting his eyes.
Then she glanced down at Merry again. "This is the
man I told you about. The one who brought me those
boxes for your playhouse."

"Oh." The little girl darted a less-shy look in his direction. "Thank you."

"You're welcome." Then Trent frowned, irritated that they'd strayed so far from his purpose.

Determined to get to it, he pinned Rebecca with an implacable stare. "Can we talk?"

She blinked a couple of times. "Oh, um, sure. But I have to stay in the playroom. I told my friend Janet I'd cover for her—we have a nurse in here at all times." She looked down and suggested to Merry that she serve herself a glass of juice and then watch TV. The little girl moved off and Rebecca reached for Vince.

He huddled back against Trent's chest. "Gawaa gawaa gawaa."

"Don't worry about it. He just needs a little guy time." Trent reassured the baby by hitching him closer.

"Are you sure?" Rebecca frowned.

"I'm used to babies."

"I can see that." She shook her head as if it surprised her.

But if she'd known his mother the way Trent did, it wouldn't. Not that he'd been the perfect parental figure, either, but he'd done his best with the younger ones when he was growing up, when his father had spent all his time at work and his mother had spent all of hers doing as little as possible for her children. Trent would do his best with the child Rebecca was carrying, too.

He followed her to a deserted corner of the playroom and waited until they'd both settled into facing, cushioned chairs. Then he broached the subject that had been weighing on him for the last forty-two, almost forty-three, hours. "What are your thoughts on my offer?"

She froze. "Your offer?"

"From the other night?"

"From the other night?"

There was either an echo in the room or she was stalling. "Rebecca—"

"Why was your sperm at Children's Connection?"

The question caught him by surprise. "Morgan Davis didn't tell you?" He'd figured the clinic's director had spilled the whole story.

She shook her head. "Only that it wasn't donated for artificial insemination purposes."

Which led him to another question of his own. "Why did you go that route, by the way? You're what—twenty-five?"

"Twenty-seven."

"Why didn't you wait until you found the right guy? Do it the old-fashioned way?"

"The old-fashioned way was out of the question. The 'right guy' divorced me two years ago."

From the cool expression on her face, Mr. Right Guy had put her right off romance. Well, it wasn't as if Trent held any faith about matches being made in heaven, either. His parents' marriage and his own had both ended with unhappiness. He ran a hand through his hair, then stared down at the blue casts binding Vince's short legs. "You sound as if you're as soured on the whole love and marriage thing as I am."

"*Are* you soured?"

He shrugged, then released a dry laugh. "Yeah. You asked why my sperm was at the clinic. My ex—my wife at the time, of course—was going to be inseminated. We thought it would increase the chances of her becoming pregnant. But when the big day came, she did the big back-out. Of my entire life."

Rebecca released a little sigh. "I've come to the conclusion that while there *are* some good marriages built on real love, those are the exception. I'm not holding out hope that a fluke will happen to me."

"Okay, so you're not looking for a man. But why a baby? Haven't you got plenty of them to occupy your time at the hospital?"

As if to emphasize his remark, Vince chose that moment to launch himself toward Rebecca. Trent passed the child over, again struck by the sweet, automatic caress she gave the baby as he settled against her. He could watch her stroke her cheek against a baby's downy head a dozen times, he thought, and never grow tired of it.

"I'm very good at my job, you know," Rebecca said.

A non sequitur? Something about the way she said the words made it clear it was not. He tilted his head. "Okay. So you're good at your job...?"

Her gaze on the baby's face, she rocked him side-to-side as he snuggled against her shoulder. "There's a need for people who can do what I do."

"I'm certain you're right, but—"

"It takes a lot out of me." Her gaze came up to meet

his, and it was both direct and vulnerable. "Sick children, all day, every day." Her voice lowered to a whisper. "Sick children, hurt children, suffering children. Dying children, Trent."

His eyes jumped to Vince, now sound asleep against Rebecca's flamingo smock. He couldn't ask what was wrong with the baby. He didn't want to know.

He couldn't imagine how Rebecca could come to work every day.

"Why?" he asked.

She seemed to understand his question. "Because I can help many, many of them get well. Because I can comfort all of them. Because…because I can."

For a second he felt ashamed that all he did was run a multimillion-dollar company. Then he cleared his throat. "But another child, Rebecca?"

Her gaze dropped from his. She lifted Vince's tiny hand and set it on top of hers, then stroked the baby's soft skin with her forefinger. "I need my own child, my own family to fill my well, Trent. To be my light, to be the strength I need to do a job that can tear me up inside. I need my own child to come home to, someone to repair the heart that gets broken a little bit every day. I need someone of my own to love."

He tried to tell himself she'd made the speech with calculation, for maximum effect. With the sound of violins playing in her imagination.

"That brings us to my offer, I suppose," he finally said.

"Your offer." She blinked at him a couple of times,

her face paling. "I thought…I was so tired, I thought I dreamed it. I couldn't believe—"

"That I'd make such a proposition?" Trent heard the flat tone in his voice. "But I did. Half a million for the baby you're carrying. And after what you just said, I'm ready to up the ante to a full seven figures."

Three

Rebecca stared at the man across from her. He didn't look like a nightmare—no, he looked like a dream—but she should be screaming all the same. "You'd give me a million dollars for my baby?"

"*Our* baby. And yes, I would give you a million, but you wouldn't accept it, would you?"

In relief, her heart tripped up, tangling her tongue, too. "I— You…" She sagged against the back of the chair, swallowed.

One of the kids at the other end of the room let out a screech, drawing Trent's attention. When he turned back to her, he said, "We need to schedule another talk. More private."

"All right." She croaked out the words, her voice still rough from surprise.

"I have something this evening I can't get out of." He rose, towering over her. "But how about tomorrow night?"

She rose, too, with Vince cradled against her in one arm. "Okay." Her mind was catching up to events. Trent had come here perfectly serious about wanting to *buy* her baby! But he was leaving now, and seemingly convinced that he couldn't, that she wouldn't agree. But did that mean he was going to relinquish his rights? That was what she wanted. That's what she needed *him* to agree upon.

Her free hand crept over her belly. *What should I do, Eisenhower?*

As she walked Trent toward the playroom's exit, her gaze landed on the poster taped to both sides of the glass door. "The fair," she said aloud.

"What?" He paused and looked at her.

If he saw her with kids again, if he got to know her a little better, he would see she'd make a good mother and that she didn't need or want anything from him. He continued to look down at her, waiting.

"Tomorrow's Saturday," she said. "If you don't have something else going on, would you…like to come help me out at the children's fair? I'm sort of half in charge and we could use an extra set of hands."

"A children's fair?" He said the words as if he'd never heard of such a thing.

Probably because the big, bad businessman usually concerned himself with big, bad business and not something as mundane as hot dogs and pony rides. She smiled at him, anyway. "You said you were good with babies."

"I did, didn't I?" Then he turned and strode for the door.

"Ten o'clock!" she called out after him. "I hope to see you there!"

By the time 9:45 a.m. rolled around, Rebecca realized she'd organized herself right out of anything major to do. Weeks ago she'd canvassed the hospital staff for volunteers and they'd stepped up without arm-twisting. The proceeds were going to benefit Camp I Can, a summer camp dear to the heart of Meredith Malone Weber, a pediatrics physical therapist. Thanks to that good cause, artistic nursing assistants were in place to paint little faces. Interns were using their rotating breaks to grill hot dogs or hand out sunscreen samples. Other volunteers were lined up to do everything from selling tickets to supervising the line for the ponies.

The flagged-off area for the fair was already starting to fill even before the official opening. Rebecca waved at a few faces she recognized, then went back to the last-minute run-through of her list. With the excited chatter and squeals of children rising around her, the hand that touched her shoulder came out of the blue at the same time that a male voice spoke in her ear. "Reporting for duty, Nurse Holley."

Trent. It was Trent. Her face heated despite herself as she glanced up and took in his damp, dark golden hair, white T-shirt and worn jeans. He wore running shoes, the expensive kind that she always thought should do the running on their own at that price tag.

"Is there something wrong with what I'm wearing?" His hand slid from her shoulder and he held both arms out.

She shook her head, thinking, *I was right about those good-looking genes, Eisenhower.* "No, you're perfect." Her face burned. "I mean, what you're *wearing* is perfect."

"You look nice, too."

Right. Her hair was pulled back in a ponytail. Her jeans, tennies and man-size Property of Portland General T-shirt was probably as unfamiliar to him as woman's wear as the scrubs he'd seen her in before. But she wasn't hoping to impress him as a *female.* Today was about showing him her maternal, responsible side.

A toddler bumped into her knees and she automatically reached down to steady the child. See? Today was about moments like this, when she could prove to him she was the right person to retain sole custody of the baby he'd unwittingly half created.

"So, what can I do?" he asked.

She ran her finger down the list on her clipboard, then grimaced. Before finalizing the assignments, maybe she should have considered what kind of job Trent Crosby, CEO, would find appropriate. "How do you feel about cotton candy?" It was the single booth not yet manned.

"The sweet, sticky stuff?"

Grimacing again, she nodded. "Sorry, but it's the only job left."

He chucked her under the chin, then leaned close, as if preparing to share a deep, dark secret. "Don't apologize." His warm breath tickled the side of her neck. "There's nothing I like better than sweet and sticky."

Rebecca's muscles froze solid as his words, his teasing tone, the closeness of him sent a wave of contrasting heat over her skin. Beneath her T-shirt, her nipples contracted into hard points, pressing against the cups of her bra. Drawing in a breath, she sucked in that delicious, spicy scent that she'd smelled on Trent's skin the night he'd half carried her to bed.

She inhaled it again, and something deep inside her, something long-dormant, stirred.

Desire, she realized. It stretched, warming up and loosening her insides.

"You okay?"

No. She hadn't wanted a man since discovering the $988.72 Victoria's Secret charge on her husband's credit card. She hadn't thought about her body in sexual terms since deciding upon becoming a mother.

"I'm fine." She would be. Some new pregnancy hormone had probably kicked in and was coursing through her bloodstream, causing this odd heaviness in her breasts and belly. It wasn't Trent who was responsible for the sudden tautness of her skin and her enhanced sense of smell.

"Let's go, then." He looked down at her, his eyebrows raised. Maybe puzzled by her strange behavior, but certainly not under the sexual spell that had paralyzed her.

"Yes, let's go." She forced herself to move. In a few

minutes her hormone levels would rebalance and she would see him as the rich, unreachable guy he was. She wouldn't *smell* him, be aware of him, want to touch him and have him touch her with such a painful ache.

Today was supposed to be about showing him she was responsible and maternal, not needy and sexual.

The cotton-candy machine was set up at the end of the aisle of food booths. The outfit they'd rented it from had provided the cartons of pink floss sugar to fill the machine as well as the paper cones to wind the candy threads around. It had looked easy during the demonstration.

"Once the machine's warmed up and spinning," she explained to Trent, as she started following her own instructions, "you just twirl the cone as you move it around the edge, picking up the cotton as you go along."

But despite the simple instructions, her effort wasn't going well. What was supposed to be a full, puffy ball of cotton candy was wispy and drooping. More of the floss coated her fingers than covered the cone. Frustrated, she stopped and studied the result. "It looks terrible."

"You better let me taste it," Trent said.

"Huh?" Frowning, she held it up for his inspection. "I don't know what's—"

His hand wrapped around her wrist.

At the contact, her arm jerked.

His mouth, which had been leaning in for that taste, sampled the sticky back of her hand instead. Warm and wet, his tongue swiped across her skin.

That new hormone flooded her again. Her gaze flew

to his, and her eyes widened as her skin prickled and her nipples tingled, then tightened, in one unstoppable, sexual rush. Could he tell?

Oh yeah, he could. His nostrils flared, as if scenting the desire oozing out of her pores.

Her voice came out a broken whisper. "I don't…I don't know…"

"You don't know what?" *His* voice was lower, raspier.

"I don't know what to say." But she had to say something, right? "I'm, uh, sorry."

"No need to apologize." Trent's eyes flicked to her mouth, and then back up. "I told you I like it sweet and sticky."

His one hand still holding on to her wrist, he lifted the other to pinch a bit of candy off the cone and held it toward her lips. "See what you think." He sounded like seduction, his voice liquid and coaxing.

Which made her *feel* liquid, sweet and sticky, and she was afraid she wasn't hiding it very well. It wasn't a maternal, responsible response. It wasn't a smart thing for him to see. It wasn't safe or smart for her to let *him,* of all people, make her feel that way.

"Come on, don't be afraid. Open up that pretty mouth and taste."

Oh, he sounded like seduction, all right. Her mouth was halfway open, her tongue halfway out.

A child's voice pierced the heated air around them. "Mama! Mama! Cotton candy! Please! Buy me cotton candy."

Rebecca lurched back. Trent's fingers released her and she spun toward the child and parent. "Can I help you?" she asked, trying to sound normal.

She must have looked normal, because the mother handed over the two tickets required instead of running in the other direction to protect her son from the X-rated thoughts rattling around in Rebecca's brain. The little boy bobbed up and down on his heels while Trent started on the candy. His first effort came out perfectly, wouldn't you know? But she didn't have a chance to commend him on it because by the time he handed it over, they had a five-deep line.

It stayed five-deep for the next couple of hours, so she didn't have time to think, let alone worry over her uncontrollable response to Trent. At his insistence, she took one quick break from the booth to eat a hot dog and drink a bottle of water—she brought the same back to him—and then, as quickly as the line had formed, it evaporated. The fair was nearly over and, from the looks of things, had been an unqualified success.

However, the dearth of customers meant Rebecca had to face Trent without anything but the cotton-candy machine between them. She had to face up to those brief, but charged moments of sexual awareness. In their booth's new silence, the whirring noise of the mechanism sounded loud, but not as loud as her beating heart. He switched off the machine, but, unwilling to meet his eyes, she kept her head down and pretended an interest in the coffee can of tickets she'd collected.

What's he going to think about me now, Eisen-

hower? What kind of responsible mom goes wild with desire over a man she barely knows? Maybe he wouldn't bring it up. And even if he did, maybe she could pretend he'd mistaken what had happened.

Yeah, right. And then he'd happen to brush against her once more and she'd melt into a puddle at his feet.

What kind of impression would that make?

"Rebecca."

Trent's voice, close by, startled her. Worried that he might touch her again, she stumbled back, knocking into the cotton-candy machine. To save herself, she reached behind, her steadying hands plunging into the remnants of gooey candy floss.

Still unbalanced, she staggered backward some more, her foot knocking over an open carton of cotton-candy mix that was still half full. As she whirled to grab the container, the powder spilled all over her tennies.

"Oh, no!" She groaned and, looking down at the mess, ran her hands over her hair—where they stuck like gum.

With another groan, she yanked them free. Aware of her appearance, and that as impressions went, she'd left an indelible one of incredible awkwardness, she raised her gaze to meet Trent's. "I can't believe this."

His lips twitched. "Maybe it's my fault. But when I said I liked sticky and sweet, I didn't mean—"

"Ooooh!"

"Don't stamp your foot when you're standing in all that powder, because then you'll have more than a mustard stain on your shirt."

Her gaze dropped. Sure enough, there was a big ol' swathe of bright yellow across the front of her T-shirt. A nice contrast to the pink cast to her sticky hands. "I'm usually a very neat person," she muttered, annoyed at his teasing and embarrassed all over again. "Seriously. Ask anyone."

He laughed. "And I'll give you the chance to prove it. Let me see if I can find a bucket of water and a broom."

"Would you?" At least that would give her a few moments alone to mourn her dignity. "Go to the ticket booth and ask for Eddie. He'll help."

"Eddie." Trent nodded, then grinned at her. "Now, don't go anywhere."

As if she could, she thought, looking at the remains of the cotton-candy booth that needed to be cleaned up. Not to mention herself. Could the day get any worse? Could she *appear* any worse in Trent's eyes?

"Well, well, well," a familiar voice said. "If it isn't my ex. And looking her usual best."

Humiliation skittered like a cockroach down Rebecca's spine. Determined not to let her former husband see her reaction, though, she lifted her chin and coolly met his gaze.

He was looking like a million and one bucks, in expensive khakis and a starched dress shirt, his initials embroidered on the pocket. His white doctor's coat was thrown over one arm and his fingers were twined with those of the woman he'd left her for—Constance Blake. In a pastel suit, Constance looked like two million and one bucks, plus all the alimony payments that Rebecca deserved but that her ex-husband had managed to weasel out of.

"Hello, Ray." He hated when she called him that. His given name was Rayburn and it was his preference. He'd always said Ray was a guy who sprawled on the couch and drank beer.

Well, better a stay-at-home beer-drinker than a cheating swiller of chardonnay who spent all his spare time sharing someone else's bed.

"Is everything okay, Rebecca?" At the new voice, they all looked over. There was Trent, lugging a bucket of water and an old straw broom.

Oh, no. Rebecca gave an inward moan. The last thing she wanted was for Eisenhower's daddy to meet Ray. That would only clinch the bad impression she'd made on Trent today. What kind of woman would ever have married such a jerk?

As if he had to confirm that fact, Ray opened his mouth. "Is this your new boyfriend, Becca?" His gaze focused on the bucket and the broom, and he smiled, except on Ray it looked like a sneer. "You dating the janitor now?"

Trent had been taking himself to task all the way to Eddie and back. Thinking with the brain below his belt instead of the one between his ears had led him to teasing and flirting with Rebecca. But she didn't need that. She'd said she didn't need or want anything from him.

He certainly didn't need to wind their accidental entanglement any tighter.

But those thoughts evaporated when he took in the man and woman talking with Rebecca. Trent didn't like that stiff expression on her face, an expression that turned even stiffer when the other man said something Trent didn't catch. Something about "the janitor."

He strode closer, then stepped over the short front wall of their booth. "Excuse me?" he said, meeting the other man's gaze. "Were you talking to me?"

The guy's eyes slid toward Rebecca. "I was asking about Becca's love life." A faint smile looked nasty on his too-pretty face.

"My love life's none of your business, Ray," Rebecca replied. She glanced over at Trent, then released a tiny sigh. "This is my ex-husband, Rayburn Holley, and his friend, Constance Blake. Ray, Constance, this is Trent Crosby."

"*Doctor* Rayburn Holley," the man said. His gaze traveled to the bucket and broom Trent carried. "I'd shake hands but I'm on duty in a few minutes. So you're making time with my little Becca, huh?"

Aaah. Now if he put love life and janitor together, it was clear that Dr. Ray had been trying to put his ex-wife down. Trent smiled. "We're making something, all right, Ray." He turned to the man's companion. "Hey there, Constance. Did your brother tell you I kicked his ass on the tennis court last week?"

If smiles could kill, Constance's would have flash-frozen him on the spot. His mother and his ex-wife had been expert at that kind of smile and he was expert at deflecting it.

He grinned back. "What's the matter, Con? Tooth-ache?"

"There's not a thing wrong with me, Trent."

"Nothing that a little warm blood wouldn't help," he murmured for Rebecca's ears only and was gratified to hear her little snort of choked-off laughter. Then he raised his voice. "My mistake. I thought maybe that's why you had an appointment with Dr. Ray here."

"I'm a *dermatologist,* not a dentist." The doctor shot a glance at his companion. "You know this man, Constance?"

She gave him a nudge with her elbow. "He's Trent Crosby, Rayburn. Of Crosby Systems?"

Dr. Ray blinked. The he looked from Rebecca to Trent. From Trent to Rebecca. "Well." He shook his head. "Well, well."

Rebecca crossed her arms over her chest. "Yes, *well,* let's not keep you, Ray. I'm sure your patients need you more than we do."

"I don't—" Ray blinked again. "So there is a 'we,' Rebecca? You and *Trent Crosby?*"

The embarrassed flush on Rebecca's face was all the impetus Trent needed. He pasted on his best man-to-man smile. "What else would get me out of the office or off the golf course on a Saturday morning but a beautiful woman, right, Ray? A beautiful, *desirable* woman." His arm looped around Rebecca's neck to draw her close. He pressed his mouth against hers in a casual kiss.

At the light contact, a fire flared. Trent jerked away

from it, staring into Rebecca's equally startled eyes. It took an effort to break her gaze and meet Dr. Ray's. "And, uh, thanks, by the way."

"For what?" The other man didn't look happy.

Trent hugged Rebecca closer. He didn't dare kiss her again. "For this woman, of course. Your loss is my gain."

It sent the supercilious bastard on his way, trailed by the Ice Queen who deserved him. Trent kept his arm around Rebecca until the other couple was out of sight.

That was when her shoulders slumped and she slid away from his embrace. "You didn't need to do that."

"What?" He couldn't help smiling at Rebecca, because Dr. SOB was out of her life and because she looked so damn cute with cotton candy in her hair.

"Pretend for Ray."

Trent shrugged. "He was trying to do a number on you."

"I know." She sighed. "I know, and I still can't help falling for it. After I caught him cheating, it was as if he blamed me for his own failings."

"Spouses are pigs."

She laughed, as he'd hoped she would. Then she sobered. "Sometimes I feel bad about being so pessimistic about love. Then again, sometimes I feel smug."

"I only feel smart."

She laughed again. "At least you're honest. Ray wasn't."

"Neither was my ex-wife."

"I suppose that means we have more in common than I would ever have suspected," Rebecca replied.

"Yeah. Cheating spouses and a lousy attitude toward love."

"There's the pregnancy, too." Rebecca's eyes bored straight into his. "And I have to be honest and up-front about it, Trent. I need to make sure you understand that I will never, ever give up my baby. I want you to give *me* sole custody."

While he'd known that was what she was after, it made him almost angry to hear her say it. "Am I such a bad guy?"

Her gaze dropped. "You're not a bad guy, no." Color stained her cheeks and she pressed her lips together.

It made him think of the kiss. That surprising burst of heat. Maybe he would be better off distancing himself permanently from her. From the baby.

But he couldn't! Memories slammed him from all sides. Chubby cheeks, little fingers, hero worship. He thought of his nephew and Robbie Logan. He couldn't lose another child. He couldn't.

"I have to be honest, too," he said. "I can't just walk away, Rebecca."

She nodded, as if he'd confirmed her worst fears. "We'll have to come up with another plan, then."

Yes, another plan. He thought they could, because, despite their initial misfires, they got along well enough. Very well, as a matter of fact. They could laugh together, enjoy each other's company, enjoy a kiss. Hell, that was more than his own parents had found in their marriage.

"Our baby should have a mother and a father in its life," he said. "Full-time."

Rebecca shrugged. "That's ideal, but not a necessity."

Trent thought of his parents' marriage again. They'd lived separate lives, for all intents and purposes, but in the same house. They'd had the children between them, along with a boatload of animosity, but what if the animosity hadn't been there? What if they could have gotten along, two separate beings who shared living space and their progeny? That could have worked.

It *could* work.

"Maybe we should get married," he said aloud, trying out the sound of it. "What do you think?"

Four

Dressed in his disguise of tattered jeans, plaid flannel shirt over a sweatshirt and Seattle Mariners baseball cap pulled low over his eyes, Everett Baker stood concealed on the other side of the flimsy, plywood back wall of the cotton-candy booth, listening to the couple inside. He knew Rebecca Holley by sight from his job as an accountant at the Children's Center. Trent Crosby he'd never met. At least not since they were children. Perhaps he should feel bad for eavesdropping on them, but eavesdropping was the least of his crimes.

The two in the booth would have other reasons to despise him.

Just as he'd begun to despise himself since he'd been on the run from the FBI.

But Nancy loves me.

He had to hold on to that. He'd already told Portland General Hospital's nurse Nancy Allen about the things he'd done, yet miraculously, she still loved him. She still believed in him.

He had to prove to her that her faith in him wasn't groundless. That there *was* a reason to love him. So leaving town was no longer an option. He had to own up to his crimes.

Though confident that no one would recognize the well-pressed bean-counter he'd been in his new grunge-guise, Everett walked behind the facades of the booths set up for the fair, where no one could see him. Even before the FBI had begun looking for him, that was how he'd lived most of his life—behind a facade, and distant from other people. Most of the time he blamed himself for that distance, it was his fault he was so shy, his fault he couldn't reach out and let people see who he really was.

Other times he realized that his childhood had forced that role and those ways upon him.

"Daddy!" Through the plywood barriers he could hear a young boy's voice. "Can we go to the park now? You promised we'd play ball today."

Play ball.

A familiar scene fluttered through his mind. He used to think it was a fantasy, or something from an old movie or television program that he couldn't remember watching. But now he knew it for what it was—a memory. A box with crinkly silver paper. More paper inside.

And inside *that,* smelling almost as good as his mother's flowery perfume, a beautiful leather baseball mitt, just his size.

Can we play ball now, Dad? Can we? Can we?

He'd loved that mitt. He'd loved baseball.

But his father had changed. His father had gone from fun and loving to foul-mouthed and stinking of booze. His mother had changed, too. And his home had never been the same.

He had never been the same. Not anything about him.

Now he found himself standing next to a payphone tucked beside one of the seldom-used side exits of Portland General. Digging through his pockets, he found some change, and without giving himself time to think about it, dialed the number. He'd memorized it from the card the detective had given him when he'd accompanied Nancy to the police station a few weeks before. Then, he'd tried to deflect her warnings about the possibility of a kidnapping ring by telling Detective Levine that the nurse was tired and overworked. He'd tried to give the police officer the impression that she was imagining things.

Now he was determined to confirm the truth of what Nancy had said. With the ringleader of their group, Charlie Prescott, found by the FBI and shot dead, Everett thought it was finally safe to do so.

"Detective Levine," a voice said over the phone.

He thought of all the people he'd hurt. He thought of all he had to regret.

"Hello? Is anyone there?" The detective sounded impatient.

He thought of Nancy. Nancy and his mother and father—the way they'd been at first. "Hello, Detective," he said. "We've spoken before. About a possible kidnapping ring."

"Who is this?" the detective barked out.

"This is—" He hesitated, then forced out the words. "This is Everett Baker. I know you and the FBI have been looking for me and I'd like to come in. I have information that you need to hear."

The evening of the children's fair, when Rebecca opened her front door to Trent, she knew he must have been kidding when he'd said "Maybe we should get married." Despite the three large, but otherwise very ordinary bags of Chinese takeout in his arms, he was too...*too* for a woman such as herself. Too rich, too good-looking, too attractive to settle for a marriage of convenience based upon unforeseen circumstances.

"Aren't you going to invite me in?" he asked.

"Oh! Oh, yes." *Oh, God.* She'd been standing in the doorway just staring at him. After making such a fool of herself at the fair, the last thing she wanted was to look ridiculous in his eyes again. She stepped aside and gestured him inside. "Let me take the food. I'll put it on plates and we can eat in the living room, okay?"

"Sure." He leaned down to transfer the bags.

She circled her arms to take them from him. It should have been simple. But in the middle of the process, they both hesitated, and Rebecca felt paralyzed by the complexity of the task. Should she grab them, or should he drop them? It was like a first kiss, she thought, all those awkward questions. Where to put the noses? Which way to turn your head?

Except they'd already shared a first kiss and it hadn't been awkward at all.

Hoping he couldn't read that latest thought on her face, she shuffled closer to him. He leaned farther forward. His forearms brushed against her breasts. Their bodies froze again.

Goose bumps shot across her chest and down her belly. She should close her arms around the bags. She should take them, then move away as if no contact had ever occurred.

Instead she held to that pose, her arms loosely circling his. His skin, bared to the elbow due to the sleeves of his rolled-up shirt, only a sweatshirt-thickness away from parts of her body that were growing heavier, achier by the heartbeat.

He cleared his throat. "Maybe I should carry these to the kitchen myself," he said and turned that way.

Heat flooded Rebecca's face. What was happening to her? The poor man probably thought *she* thought he'd been serious about that joking proposal and that she was now eager to cement the deal with sex. She hurried after him, determined to put his mind at ease. "Look, I…"

In the kitchen, he was studying a framed photo collage of her family mounted on the wall beside the counter where he'd placed the bags. "Your people?" he asked, glancing over at her.

"My people?" she echoed, drawing closer to stand

alongside him and gaze at the montage of smiling faces. Her finger reached out to brush a speck of dust off the image of her mother. It had been the last Christmas she was alive. "Yes. My people."

"They live nearby?"

She shook her head. "We're scattered all over the country. I don't think we've been all together for a holiday since these were taken. My mom had cancer and we wanted to make it one last memorable Christmas." Grief tore a new hole in her heart.

What I wouldn't give to have my mom around right now. And to talk to her about the baby.

"What would she say?"

Rebecca started and jerked her gaze to Trent. "Did I speak out loud?"

He half smiled and drew the back of his forefinger down her cheek. "Afraid so."

She frowned at him, hoping it would disguise the new heat on her face. "You make the oddest things to happen to me."

That finger made another slow meander down her skin. "Yeah? Well, I'm beginning to regret not being there when the oddest thing I did to you happened."

That took her a second to decipher. Once she did, she saw the spark of teasing in his eyes. "Oh, you!" She whacked his shoulder, just as if he was one of her hulking little brothers pictured inside the frame, and then bustled toward the counter to set out the food.

She felt him watching her. "What would she say?" he asked again.

"My mom?" With her attention focused on dishing out the chow mein, it wasn't so hard to speak about it. "She'd be thrilled that I was pregnant. She always told me I'd make a great mother."

"What would she think of me as a father? As your husband?"

Rebecca looked up and was struck by the serious expression on his face. "I—I don't know."

"I was sincere about us getting married, Rebecca."

The serving spoon clattered onto the counter. "No, you weren't."

"Oh, but I was." He crossed over to her and she backed away. But instead of pressing forward, he took over the doling out of the food. "And here's your fair warning—I always get what I want."

"You don't want me!" How could he? How could this tall, gorgeous man, who was so competently filling their plates—so *calmly* filling their plates— want to be her husband?

He refolded the flaps of the last carton, then took both plates in hand and led the way back to the living room, where she'd set places on the narrow coffee table in front of the love seat. As she seated herself, he followed suit.

Then he said, in that casual, calm way of his, "I *want* this baby." With a practiced flip, he snapped open her folded cloth napkin and placed it in her lap. Then he put a fork into her nerveless fingers. "I won't settle for anything less than being our baby's father."

Our baby. That tore at her heart, too.

"Eat up," Trent admonished, then set to his own meal with relish.

She could only stare at him. He thought he could say these things—*marriage, our baby*—without them affecting her appetite? He could say them, be thinking them, without them affecting *his* appetite?

But then she noticed he was merely stirring around his food, not actually putting any of it in his mouth. She narrowed her gaze. This was how he operated in business, she'd bet. Calmly, coolly, telling you what he wanted, what he was going to do, and then going ahead and acting on it as if you were willing to follow right along. Well! Rebecca Holley wasn't such an easy mark.

He gave her a sidelong look. "You're not going to buy right into this, are you?"

That he so easily read her mind startled her into laughing. "No, I'm not."

He shrugged. "It was worth a try. It's a business tactic that will work if the opposition already wants to give what I'm asking for. I get a better deal and they convince themselves later they were steamrollered into it."

"Well, you're not going to steamroller me." It wasn't lost on her that the first tactic he'd chosen was the one he'd use on someone who already wanted to give what he was asking for. Apparently she *had* looked easy to him. She knew she had, darn it.

Rebecca forked up a bite of orange chicken and popped it into her mouth. With a small smile, he turned his attention to his own plate and really started eating this time. Rebecca speared another bite of food and let her silence speak for itself.

By the time this evening was over, Trent Crosby was going to find out that Rebecca Holley had a spine of steel, not to mention pride.

He didn't try any more maneuvers on her as they finished their meal and cleared away the dishes. Then she made two after-dinner cups of green tea and carried them out to the love seat. Trent was holding a fortune cookie in each hand. "You choose," he said, as she settled down beside him again, bending one leg beneath her body.

She took one, broke it open, read it aloud. "'Help! I'm a prisoner in a fortune-cookie factory.' I always get that one."

He laughed, then broke his. The little slip of paper fluttered to the ground between them. They both leaned forward, reached for it. Her hand found it first, his hand found hers.

Rebecca heard herself gasp.

"What is it? What's wrong?" He straightened up, frowning at her.

"A...a charley horse." She had to say something, didn't she? It probably *was* some sort of cramp, something like that, anyway, that jolted through her at his touch.

"Let me rub it for you."

"Oh, no, no!" But he was already tugging on that leg bent beneath her, and the sensation of his fingers on her again was sending her common sense skittering all over the galaxy. Before she could gather it back up, her calf was in his lap and his long fingers were massaging her leg over the thick material of her sweatpants. He tipped off the backless tennies she was wearing to cup her heel in his hand.

"Your feet are cold."

"Really?" They should be hot with all the blood that was leaving her brain and heading to points south. When he rubbed his knuckles against the arch of her foot, her fingers curled. The crackle of paper reminded her she still held his fortune in her hand.

Focusing on it instead of the seductive warmth of his touch, she read it aloud. "'The truth will set you free.'"

He grimaced. "There's another original one." His hands continued making their magic.

Rebecca told herself that it was natural for a woman who took care of others all day long to want to moan when a man bothered to take care of her. When he lifted her other foot into his lap, she didn't protest. She was getting used to his hands on her now, the electrical shock of it turning to a pleasant, almost drowsy buzz.

"But maybe the truth will set me free," she heard him muse aloud.

"Hmm?" She looked at him through half-closed eyes. Her full cup of tea was on the table beside her, but it felt as if she'd already sipped it down, because her insides were warm and soft.

"Maybe it would help persuade you if I tell you why our baby is so important to me."

Our baby. The words didn't alarm her, didn't tear at

her heart as they had before. The busy day, his massaging fingers, the warm food in her belly were making her sleepy, that bone-deep sleepiness that she'd felt the other time he was here. "Why?" she almost whispered it. "Why is the baby so important to you?"

"I can't lose another child."

That cleared some of the cobwebs taking over her mind. "Another child? What do you mean, you can't lose *another* child?"

"Shh, shh." He patted her knee with one hand, even as the other continued kneading the back of her calf. "It's just that...I was the oldest, okay? And my mother...she relied on me for a lot. Frankly, she must have flunked Maternal Feelings 101, but that's beside the point."

Rebecca relaxed against the arm of the love seat. "What is the point, Trent?"

"The point is, when I was nine years old, my little brother Danny had a friend over. They were both six. We were playing outside. My mom didn't like us spending too much time indoors. She was somewhere, on the phone or something, and Danny and his friend Robbie had a motorized airplane they were fooling around with. I was shooting hoops and my little sister Katie—"

"She was playing with you?"

He shook his head. "She was just a baby. I had her in the stroller outside with me."

So Trent was a built-in baby-sitter for Mama Crosby who didn't like her kids indoors. Rebecca grimaced. She'd seen the type before. "And then what happened?"

Trent looked over as if he'd forgotten she was there. "The airplane got stuck in a tree. Danny went inside to ask Mom for help. I kept playing basketball."

"With Katie there beside you."

"Yes, with Katie there beside me. And then…Robbie wandered into the front yard. From the house my brother saw him talking to a stranger, but by the time he alerted our mom, both the stranger and Robbie Logan were gone."

"The Logans." A chill entered all that delicious warmth inside her. "I recall hearing something about their oldest son being kidnapped. But never found, right?"

"That's right." Trent's jaw hardened. "But his remains were found."

Rebecca's stomach clenched. "But you know you weren't responsible. You couldn't have—"

"I could have done something if I'd been watching them more closely. If I'd followed them into the front yard—"

"But you were watching the baby! It wasn't your fault, Trent."

He laughed, a short, cold sound. "I know. I think I even was able to forget about it for a little while until Danny's little boy, my nephew, was kidnapped."

Rebecca stared. "No!"

"Yes." Trent's expression grew remote. "Four years ago, when he was a year old. His mother, my sister-in-law, killed herself a year after that."

"Oh, God." Now Rebecca could understand how loss

like this had become such a monster in Trent's eyes. In his heart. She curled her legs out of his lap and knelt on the cushions beside him. "I'm sorry, Trent." Her hands grasped both of his. "I'm so sorry for your family's pain."

Though his fingers laced with hers, his expression remained distant. "I want to be in this baby's life." His voice wasn't urgent or upset. It wasn't cool and casual, either. It was plain certain. "Our baby's life."

Oh, no. She felt her spine going soft. "Trent…"

"I want an arrangement that won't make it easy for you to take the baby from me."

"I wouldn't—"

"And I don't want to be a part-time father either. I've had one of those, too."

Rebecca stilled. "I don't want to be a part-time mother myself. That's not what I went through this for."

"If we don't get married, the fact is, Rebecca, we'll both be part-time parents. I'll make sure of that."

Jerking her hands from his, she drew away from him. "Are you threatening to take my baby from me?"

"No. I'm *telling* you that I'm going to be in this child's life. I'm *telling* you that if we share custody, then neither of us gets what we want. The only way for that to happen, for us both to be satisfied, is to get married."

She couldn't… She wouldn't…. But his determination to be a father to her baby made his offer just the teeniest bit tempting. *Oh, Eisenhower, he must love you. He must already love you like I do.* Then she remembered her steely spine. "Trent, no."

But he must have seen that sentimental yes on her face. "Don't worry, Rebecca. I promise it won't be a problem. You'll have a say in everything, in every way we work it out."

"But how could it work out? What if one day you fall in love—"

"Don't make me laugh. We're cynical on romance, remember? The fact is, we'll do better creating a partnership on practical matters. You're not counting on love to come your way, are you?"

"Hah." Then she collapsed against the back of the love seat, unable to believe what she couldn't be seriously contemplating. "This is just a bad dream, right? Tell me that any minute I'm going to wake up."

"Shh, shh, shh." He dragged her feet back into his lap and started that hypnotizing massage again. "Just relax."

She closed her eyes to give herself a barrier against his gorgeous face. "I haven't agreed," she reminded him.

"I think we should marry as soon as possible," he murmured. "There's no reason to wait and there's every reason for us to become better acquainted."

The whole idea of getting better acquainted through marriage was so overwhelming that she couldn't find the voice to protest. He kept up that soft kneading, that soft talking, spinning tales of their future that began to sound like bedtime stories.

The deep fatigue that had been hovering now settled over her like a warm blanket. She drifted off to the sound of his voice and the fairy tales he was whispering in her ear.

Later, she stirred, and discovered she was in her bedroom, fully dressed beneath the afghan her mother had made. When she reached to pull it higher, her hand encountered a piece of paper. A note. The fact that she could read it made her suddenly aware that it was morning.

And she was suddenly aware that Trent had steamrollered her, after all.

The note was a list of items she'd apparently agreed to after all.

1. Wedding date: Thursday, 3:00 p.m., County Courthouse
2. Blood test: Monday morning
3. Lawyer's office: Thursday, 2:00 p.m. to sign prenup agreement.

She remembered insisting on that.

It went on from there.

Well, she wasn't going to follow instructions. Of course she wasn't! She remembered his voice rumbling in the darkness the night before, remembered him tucking her into bed. She didn't believe it was a reasonable solution to marry Trent Crosby, even if he was as disillusioned about love as she.

The whole idea was ridiculous and she wasn't even the

slightest bit tempted, no matter how good-looking, how persuasive, how skilled he was at the kind of foot massages that a nurse would love to grow accustomed to.

To emphasize that fact, she tossed the note aside. Another little piece of paper fluttered into the air like a feather. Rebecca caught it. Stared at it.

The fortune. *And the truth shall set you free.*

Okay, the truth: She was a little bit tempted.

Fine. More than a little bit.

Was she free now?

The phone beside her bed rang. She picked it up.

"Hello, fiancée," Trent said in her ear.

Good Lord, she thought, as his voice sent a warm tickle down her malleable spine. *Not free. Not free at all.*

Five

"Admit it. You know we made a mistake. You know *you* made a mistake."

Trent looked into Rebecca's anxious face as the elevator descended another floor. "You're kidding, right? We've been married less than ten minutes. We haven't even made it out of the courthouse yet. How could this be a mistake already?"

"I'm dressed in my *nurse's uniform.* What bride starts a marriage dressed in hospital scrubs?"

"A bride who was called in for an extra shift and who couldn't find it in herself to say no, it was her wedding day, that's who. And for the record, that's *your* mistake, not mine."

"But this was all your idea, and—" She cut off the

rest of her remark as the elevator doors swished open and a trio of people stepped inside.

And I'll be damned if I say it was a mistake, Trent thought. It was the best solution to their problem for all the reasons he'd already given her. Plus, it didn't feel like a mistake. The knowledge that he was married to Rebecca gave him all the pleasures of a bulging bank account and a successful business negotiation rolled into one. There was that distinct sense of security, as well as the edgy thrill of a chase brought to a satisfying conclusion. And then, just below the surface was that intriguing simmer of possibility. It was just as he'd planned, Trent thought as they exited the elevator and walked toward their parked cars.

He slanted another look at Rebecca and put every ounce of determination and certainty into his voice. "Believe me, Rebecca, this is *not* a mistake."

"I'm not convinced you're the type of man who would ever admit to one," she grumbled.

Well, that was true. And he was also the type of man, who, when he decided he wanted something, got it by going after it in a systematic, methodical fashion. Paying attention to the details was the secret to his success and the source of his confidence. If he personally made sure that all the *t*'s were crossed and the *i*'s dotted, then any kind of acquisition was accomplished smoothly.

To his satisfaction.

Just like today.

He held to that happy thought until the moment the

two of them stood on the slate front porch of his house. With his hands gripping her suitcases, he stalled a moment before setting them down to locate his keys and release the lock. "I, uh, hope you'll like the place."

Instead of looking at her, he stared at the heavy, ugly door. What was he saying? She was going to hate it. *He* hated it. He'd bought it, furnished, right after his divorce from a guy who'd bought it, furnished, right after *his* divorce, from another guy who'd…and so on. Something like five iterations of thirty-something, just-single men had lived in the place, and it always held the cold chill of a house in which the furnace was rarely turned on. Even less pleasant, it reeked of layers of Pledge and Windex and Lysol, applied by a succession of faithful housekeepers who for years had polished surfaces that the succession of busy bachelors rarely dirtied.

Hell. Impatient with his uncharacteristic hesitation, he dropped the suitcases and dug for his keys. He swung open the door and she immediately stepped across the threshold.

Hell, he thought again. *Should I have carried her over it?* For all his planning, he hadn't thought that one out. And now it was too late. Annoyed with himself for the oversight, he retrieved the suitcases and followed her inside.

She paused in the foyer, looking around her.

A white-carpeted, sunken living room on the right. Curving staircase to the upper floor directly ahead. On the left, a dining area, then the entry to a stainless-steel kitchen and un-cozy den. As always, everything in sight gleamed, from the lacquer furniture in the living room to the red waxy tulips in the austere crystal vase precisely centered on the dining-room table.

"What do you think?" he heard himself ask.

Did he sound anxious? He hoped to God he didn't sound anxious. He didn't feel anxious, damn it, not about anything, and her doubts were kept at bay by his confidence.

"It looks…"

He *wasn't* holding his breath.

"It looks…

He was breathing, of course he was.

"…clean."

His air exhaled on a laugh; he couldn't help himself. "It's awful. I know it's awful."

"I didn't mean—"

"No, no. Don't try to backpedal now." The laughter eased the trace of tension that had found its way inside him. "'Clean' is about the nicest thing I can think to say about it, too."

She made a face at him. "It's not that bad."

"Let's admit it's bad. Let's admit it has all the charm of the inside of a coffee can."

"Trent." She shook her head. "Why are you living here if you don't like it?"

He shrugged. "It didn't matter before. It was just me and…it didn't matter where I lived. I spend most of my time at the office."

Doubt flared in her eyes again.

"But I'm going to change all that," he hurried to say. "With the baby, with you, I'm going to be spending more time at home." He gestured with one of the suitcases, worried that if he set them down she'd grab them back up and run for her life.

Of course he wasn't worried. Not really. The *i*'s, the *t*'s—he'd thought everything through with precision, right? If he kept steady, then she would too. Still, he headed for the staircase, determined to get her things farther into his space.

Just follow my lead, he thought, willing her after him.

"We can buy a new house or change this place, you know," he said, steadily mounting the stairs. "Enlarge the rooms by taking a can opener to them or something. Donate the furniture to a home for indigent monkeys."

Now she laughed. "Indigent monkeys?"

"Because the stuff is indestructible. Believe me. I spent one Saturday night amusing myself by trying to put a dent in the coffee table with everything from a Sam Adams beer bottle to a construction-quality sledgehammer. There's still not a mark on it."

"I would have supposed you spent your Saturday nights in more interesting ways than that."

He paused on the stair landing and stared down at…his wife. Since his divorce, he'd had his share of women. But none of them was interesting, he realized. Not in the way that Rebecca, with her wavy hair and valentine face, wearing her cartoon-printed hospital scrubs, was interesting to him.

Alarm edged down his back. *What the hell did that mean?*

It meant none of them had carried his baby, idiot.

Despite that calm, cool voice of reason in his head, his feet were still slow taking the stairs, so slow that she caught up with him. At the top, he gestured toward the open gallery space. "My home office, but feel free to use it if you'd like."

She nodded, then headed toward the short hallway on the right. "And the bedrooms are here?"

"Yes. I thought—" He froze as she glanced over at him.

"You thought?" she prompted.

"Th-th-the…" He was stuttering! *Stuttering!* "The first room, in front of you, I thought might make a nice nursery. It gets the morning sunlight and is closest to the stairs. Or maybe that's bad, to be so close to the stairs? And the morning light might wake the baby too early or…"

Terrific. Now he was babbling. Ultraconfident, just-follow-my-lead Trent Crosby was babbling.

"Are you all right?" Rebecca asked, frowning.

"Of course I'm all right." This was his idea, wasn't it? This whole marriage thing was his idea, his grand, well-devised, completely-thought-out, completely-the-right-idea, completely-not-a-mistake plan.

"Then that seems like a fine room for the baby," Rebecca said. "So where am I to sleep?"

The million-dollar question. The one that had pulled that self-assured rug from beneath his feet just seconds before. The one that had only occurred to him when she'd said the common, ordinary word *bedrooms.*

"Trent?" She was looking worried again, and she moved toward him. "What's the matter?"

Her nearness only made his sudden discomfiture worse. His fingers loosened on the handles of her suitcases and they plunked to the ground. She took one of his hands between both of hers. Noticing the platinum band on her fourth finger didn't help matters. Smelling her didn't help matters. Shouldn't a nurse smell like Band-Aids and iodine? Something boring and practical like that?

Rebecca smelled sweet, a light, powdery, sweet scent.

He wondered if her skin tasted sweet.

He knew her mouth did.

She was staring up at him with those innocent, baby-doll eyes, and he felt like a lecher because she was the mother of his child and he was getting hard thinking about her skin, her mouth and what her hair would look like loose around those breasts of hers he'd never seen, really had never had the chance to even judge beneath the tentlike clothes she wore. He was a lecher, all right.

And a loser. Because he'd failed in devising a way to accomplish one very important part of this whole marriage idea of his. How could he have been so stupid? When he'd proposed their practical marriage, he hadn't meant it to be a chaste one. There had been enough of a sexual simmer between them for him to know a physical relationship with her wouldn't be a hardship.

But in all his hurry to get her to the altar, he'd never broached the idea with Rebecca. It seemed a bit crass to bring it up now.

Which meant Mr. Cross-the-*t*'s and Dot-the-*i*'s *had* made a mistake. He'd never planned exactly how to get his wife into his bed.

Without specifying her reasons, Rebecca had requested a few days off, but on the day following her marriage she was back at Portland General for a meeting of a group that had become close to her heart. Months ago she'd been asked to give a talk on pediatric first aid for the Parent Adoption Network of Children's Connection. That day she'd discovered that the group was much more than an organization of parents who had adopted or were considering adoption. It was, in fact, a supportive group of individuals that included couples who had used the fertility services of Children's Connection as well. It was at that meeting that the idea of using a sperm donor had surfaced in Rebecca's mind.

Now she attended the meetings regularly, ostensibly as a health-care "consultant," but she got back in camaraderie and caring just as much as she gave in professional advice. When she was ready to announce her pregnancy, her friends in PAN would be the first she'd tell.

And they would be the first she'd tell about her marriage to Trent Crosby, too. That was if she didn't decide to call it quits first.

Rebecca paced through the hospital corridors, reassured by their familiarity. The days between finding that handwritten list on her quilt to finding herself in front of a county marriage clerk had passed in a blur. Trent had listened to her doubts, her cautions, her reasoning, and he'd countered every objection she'd had with something of his own that appeared to make even more sense.

She'd come to like him—she'd liked him nearly from the first—and the idea of entering into a marriage for all the sensible reasons he suggested had started to seem not so crazy, after all. He'd even managed to calm her mild panic immediately following the brief wedding ceremony. But then she'd entered that walk-in freezer he called a house and her worries had come rushing back. A night in a strange, bare guest room hadn't alleviated a one.

Could she and Trent really make this family plan of theirs work? If not, the time to back out was sooner, not later.

"You look as if the world is weighing on your shoulders."

With a start, Rebecca realized she'd made her way to the room where the PAN meeting was scheduled. Morgan Davis, the director of Children's Connection, was acting as greeter and he was gazing down at her with a wry expression on his face.

"Rebecca, you can't know how much I regret—"

She stopped him by putting a hand on his arm. "Morgan, we've been through the apologies." Though she wasn't prepared to tell him how she and Trent had resolved their problem—she wasn't confident their way was going to work—she didn't want to rehash the circumstances, either. She tried on a bright smile. "What's up for today? Don't we have a school psychologist coming in?"

"Canceled at the last minute." The grin on Morgan's face said he didn't find it a tragedy, however. "We're going to have an impromptu celebration instead."

"What? Why?"

He shook his head. "Mum's the word until everyone else arrives. Go on in and help yourself to refreshments."

With a backward glance at him, she followed instructions. As usual, there were cookies and drinks set on a counter, but more puzzling was the fancy sheet cake in the middle of the room. Swirled white frosting and blue-icing roses were piled high upon it in an elaborate decoration.

Sydney Aston, mother to adopted five-year-old Nicholas, walked up to stand beside Rebecca. She glanced at the cake, then glanced at Rebecca. "That looks like a wedding cake," she said in a teasing voice. "Do you have something to tell us?"

Rebecca's gaze whipped toward the other woman. "What? No! I mean, no, I didn't bring the cake in."

Sydney grinned at her. "But yes, you have something to tell us?"

Rebecca's face burned. "I, um, I…" She tried imagining the words she would use. *Trent Crosby and I… Yesterday, Trent Crosby and I… I'm married to Trent Crosby.*

"Hey, hey, hey." Sydney's grin died. "I was just kidding around, not trying to make you miserable."

But that was how Rebecca felt. Miserable. How could she and someone like Trent Crosby, CEO, make things work between them? Her hand crept over her stomach. *Eisenhower, I have to get us out of this mess.*

"Come on," Sydney took her arm and led her toward a nearby table. "You sit down and I'll bring you something hot to drink. It looks as if we're almost ready to start."

Rebecca noticed the room had filled. She waved to a few friends and then managed a smile for Sydney when she sat down beside her with two disposable cups of fragrant herbal tea. "I'm sorry, Sydney. My mind is scattered today. How are you and my darling friend Nicholas?"

"Darling Nicholas is more darling by the day." Sydney's sigh sounded bittersweet. "I never knew how much I could love him and—" She glanced over at Rebecca and there was the glint of tears in her eyes. "You'll think I'm silly."

Rebecca touched her friend's shoulder. "I won't."

"I get so afraid sometimes that someone will come along and take him away from me."

"I understand." Patting the other woman's shoulder, Rebecca felt her own eyes sting. Knowing Sydney's story—the baby had been abandoned by a former college friend who had been staying with her and that Sydney had applied to be the baby's foster mother and then later adopted him—only made the voiced fear more poignant. "It's common to feel that way, you know that from what we've heard at our meetings here. It's natural and not silly whatsoever."

Rebecca couldn't imagine losing Eisenhower. The baby was so real to her already. And wanting the best for her child was why she'd agreed to marry Trent. But could they make it work?

"It's worse because of these nightmares that Nicholas keeps having," Sydney went on to say. "He wakes up screaming and all he can tell me is that someone is taking him bye-bye. When I ask him who, he just shakes his head and starts crying."

"Someone taking him bye-bye?" Rebecca questioned. Five-year-old Nicholas was usually more articulate than that.

Sydney nodded, her gaze trained on her cup of tea. "It seems strange to me, too, because he hasn't used the phrase *bye-bye* since he was a toddler. It's as if the nightmares cause him to regress...or he's remembering something that actually happened."

"Oh, surely not, surely—"

"Can we bring the meeting to order?"

Rebecca shot Sydney another sympathetic glance, but didn't continue as the chatter in the room ceased. Morgan, wearing that big smile again, took his place at the front of the room near the fancy cake.

"Are you trying to break our diets?" one of the male PAN members called from the back of the room. "I promised my wife I'd lose my spare tire by the time our baby arrives and you're not helping, Morgan."

The crowd laughed. Morgan, too. "Today is not the day for diets," he said. "Today is a day to celebrate, because one of our own is home, safe and sound."

Rebecca looked around, noting that everyone else was doing the same. Then, from the hallway outside the room, came the plaintive cry of a baby who had been jostled out of sleep. All heads whipped toward the door.

In walked a smiling couple, a baby in the woman's arms. The man turned to grasp the elbow of a teenage girl following behind them, then he brought her forward so he could wrap one arm around the teen and the other around his wife.

"Here they are!" Morgan's voice was jubilant. "Brian and Carrie Summers and Lisa Sanders. And this little guy is Timothy Jacob who was recovered this past week, safe and unharmed!"

The room erupted in sound. Rebecca and Sydney looked at each other, then jumped up to share an exuberant hug. It was unbelievable. It was uplifting. Rebecca knew the entire staff at Portland General would be celebrating today.

With very good reason. At the end of January, Lisa Sanders had given birth early in the morning to the baby boy she'd agreed to let the Summerses adopt. But then, a little over twelve hours later, the infant had been kidnapped from the hospital nursery, despite rigorous procedures and security codes. While cameras had caught the perpetrator on tape, he had likely been disguised. No one had recognized the man. No one had called in about ransom or even a legitimate tip about where the baby could be. No one had said it out loud, but everyone had doubted that the baby would be found. Until now.

Both Rebecca and Sydney rushed over to join the others thronging the newcomers. Shouts of excitement and congratulations rang throughout the room, along with the startled cry of the baby. Rebecca noted that Carrie Summers was trying to comfort the sleepy, fussing child as well as take in all the congratulatory hugs and kisses. Catching her eye, Rebecca made a little "gimme" gesture. "I'll stay right beside you," she said, moving closer to the other woman. She knew the Summerses wouldn't want the baby out of their sight.

After a brief hesitation, Carrie gave her a grateful smile and then passed over the bundle of warm, agitated baby. Rebecca tucked the child's head beneath her chin, holding him close to her chest, and began to rock with slow movements. The baby let out another cry, dug his forehead against her neck, then snuffled into quiet as his thumb found his mouth.

Rebecca kept her breathing calm and even, in time with her side-to-side movement. Timothy pushed his head one more time against her throat, then settled into sleep.

Carrie Summers looked over and rubbed the baby's back with one hand while reaching for the teenager with the other. "We're going to be okay now," she told the group. Her gaze met her husband's. "Our family is going to be okay."

Rebecca continued holding the child as Brian sketched out the goings-on of the past few days. A man had turned himself in to the police and subsequently told them where they could find Timothy—at the home of a woman who lived in the countryside outside of Portland. At that remote location, the baby had been found in the care of a woman who had other children of her own. Timothy, thank God, had been well cared for and was in excellent health. The few details Brian was at liberty to share were quickly wrapped up as big squares of cake were being passed about the room.

"Lisa will continue living with us for as long as she likes," Brian said. "She's enrolled in the summer session of college right now, and we'd like her always to be as much a part of our family as Timothy."

Now even Lisa managed to address the smiling crowd. "Thank you, thank you all for your support and belief that the baby would be found and returned to Brian and Carrie. To us."

Brian reached for the baby, and as Rebecca handed him over she stepped back to appreciate the view of the reunited family. Brian and Carrie finally together with the child they had longed for and thought lost. Lisa, who now had people to love her, a family who wanted to take her as well as her baby into their lives.

It wasn't the traditional family setup, but it looked like a happy ending to Rebecca.

Later, she walked out of the meeting room and down the corridor with Sydney. They glanced at each other and grinned. "A good day," Sydney said.

"A very good day," Rebecca replied. "I feel as if I've hitched a ride on an ascending balloon."

Sydney nodded. "Families can begin many different ways, but the happiness always feels the same, doesn't it?"

Those words didn't leave Rebecca's mind as she headed for Trent's home. After today's PAN meeting, optimism and joy filled her heart. She refused to let her doubts hold her back any longer. It was time to start her life as Trent's wife.

Trent spent his first day as a newly married man not thinking about being newly married. Every time it crept into his thoughts, he booted it out with a kick worthy of David Beckham. At some point he was going to have to mention the change in his marital status to his co-workers and family members, but he decided that giving himself and Rebecca a few days to settle into the idea themselves was fair.

By the time he drove home, it was after seven o'clock. A mix of pride and relief coursed through him as he realized that, though his schedule had been full, newlywed or not, he'd accomplished everything on it and more. As he pulled into his driveway and caught sight of Rebecca's car, it was good to know that being married to her hadn't affected him at all. And that was the way it was going to stay, he decided.

The notion of sleeping with her had been a natural one, but he would put that on the back burner. The crucial step had been to get her married to him so that their baby was cemented into his life. He'd get through the next indefinite period of time the same way he'd gotten through today—by not letting this change in his marital situation affect his life or his routine.

Meanwhile, Rebecca was totally moved in—in one of the spare bedrooms.

He locked up the car, contemplating the evening ahead. A cold beer, and then he'd call the restaurant on 16th Street that knew his standing takeout dinner order—medium-rare T-bone steak, baked potato, hold anything the least bit green. There was the latest *Sports Illustrated* in his briefcase and he'd peruse that over his meal.

The smell was the first thing he noticed when he unlocked the front door. It seemed to grab him by the tie and tug him through the pristine dining room and into the kitchen.

Which wasn't the least bit pristine. He stared about the granite countertops—what he could see of them, anyway—taking in all the items scattered about. The least surprising item in the kitchen was Rebecca herself, who had one foot on a chair and one knee beside the sink as she reached for something on the upper shelf of a cabinet.

"Good evening." Looking down at him from her perch, her face was flushed and her waist was wrapped in one of those thin towels used to dry dishes. "How was your day?"

"My day was…" He shook his head. "What do I smell?"

"Apple cobbler."

"Apple cobbler." He repeated the words to himself. "And what's that?" He pointed to a covered pan atop the stove.

"Chicken casserole."

"And that? And that? And what about that?" His finger roamed around the room.

"Parsley. Broccoli. Green beans. The remains of them, anyway. They all went into the casserole." Her face flushed deeper. "I'm not one of those clean-as-you-go cooks."

"You made yourself dinner."

She climbed down from the counter holding a clear glass pitcher in her hand. "I made *us* dinner. I, uh, wasn't sure when you'd be home, so I made something that I could warm when you arrived."

"You didn't need to cook for me. I was going to order a takeout steak from DeLuce's."

"Oh. Well." She turned her back and hustled toward the refrigerator. "If you'd prefer that—"

"No, no. It's just that I didn't expect—I didn't think—" Apple cobbler. Chicken casserole. He'd died and gone to Leave-it-to-Beaver heaven.

"I've been thinking a lot today. About our marriage."

His gustatory delight slipped down a notch. She'd been thinking a lot about their marriage, while he'd been working on not thinking about it at all. "Listen, Rebecca, I've been giving it some thought, too." About two seconds' worth. "I don't want our…arrangement to, uh, overly impinge on either one of our lives or routines."

"Exactly!" She beamed a smile that had him thinking about heaven again. "Why don't you wash up for dinner and we can discuss it over our meal?"

So much for *Sports Illustrated*. When he made it

back to the place that she'd set for him at the kitchen table, he realized that she poured him a glass of ice water instead of the cold beer he'd been dreaming of.

"Does everything look okay?" she asked.

What was he supposed to do—complain? "Everything looks great," he assured her, pulling out her chair so that she could sit down. The green stuff in the casserole he could pick around, right? Plus, he would say anything to get cobbler at the end of the day.

They ate the first few bites in silence, except for his effusive compliments to the cook. This marriage thing might affect his life, after all, he conceded, but a woman making him good meals was nothing to worry about.

He was enjoying his second helping of chicken casserole when she reached beneath her place mat and pulled out some notebook paper. "So, as I said, I did a lot of thinking today and here's what I came up with."

"Hmm?" He cocked his head to try and read her handwriting upside down.

Laundry, grocery shopping, meal preparation and housekeeping duties," she said.

She did *laundry*, too? He'd cheerfully forego making his weekly haul to Hagan's Dry Cleaning and Laundry, though he supposed expecting her to starch and iron his shirts was too much to ask. "This sounds—"

"I've written it all up. I thought you could make dinner on Mondays, Wednesdays and Thursdays. I'll take Tuesdays, Fridays and Sundays. That leaves Saturdays for whatever."

He just stared at her, so she continued.

"On to laundry. I'll wash all my personal things, but I can put both of our other stuff, jeans and that sort, through the washer and dryer if you'll fold them and put them away. Sundays are good for that."

Sundays are good for the morning newspaper and ball games on TV.

"I've posted a grocery list on the refrigerator and I stocked up on a lot of things today, so I think we'll make it until we can get back to the store on Saturday. Now, I don't mind getting the trash into the can if you don't mind getting the can onto the street. What day does the garbage truck come? And would you prefer to dust or vacuum? I think we can each take care of our own bathrooms, right?"

The garbage truck? Dusting? Vacuuming? Cleaning *bathrooms?* "I, uh...Rebecca, I think you don't understand the, um, setup here. I have a housekeeper who comes in three times a week. I, uh, we, don't need to worry about any of the cleaning. She'll do the laundry, too, if you leave it out—though most of the time I forget and end up dropping it over at Hagan's."

"Oh." She looked down at the paper in front of her, then crumpled it up. "I see."

"As for grocery shopping and the whole meal thing, I do takeout unless I have a business dinner. I don't think a schedule like you're suggesting would work out."

"Oh," she said again, as she balled another piece of paper in her hand. She stood up. "I think I'll go to my room for a while. I'll take care of the dishes in a little bit. Don't touch a thing."

He supposed that included the apple cobbler, Trent thought with a sigh, watching her rush from the room. Not that he felt much like eating it anymore, not with those emotions he felt bubbling off the surface of her.

A door snicked shut upstairs and Trent took that as his signal to head up after her. He'd done something wrong, said something wrong, definitely screwed up somehow, and if he didn't rectify it, then this marriage would most certainly affect him and his routine.

He wouldn't be able to live with himself.

Six

Rebecca surprised Trent by answering his knock on her bedroom door with a composed, "Come in."

He pushed the door open to find her sitting against the pillows of the double bed with needles and yarn in her lap. "What do you have there?"

Her gaze was trained on the small bundle of fuzzy yellow fiber. "Most likely, a mess. But I'm trying to learn how to knit."

He shook his head in admiration. "Is there anything you can't do?"

She looked up and caught his gaze. "Maybe I can't be Trent Crosby's wife."

There she went again, damn it, thinking this was a mistake. "Rebecca…"

"Really, Trent. Housekeepers, business dinners. I don't come from that world. I don't belong in it."

"How do you know?"

"Remember Dr. Ray?"

Thinking about the jackass made Trent's teeth clench. "I remember him just fine."

"We broke up because I didn't fit in with his life."

"You're a nurse, for God's sake. He's a doctor. That sounds like a fit to me." Not that he even liked saying it.

"I didn't fit in with his *social* life. The group that he associated with after hours, people who'd attended prep schools and prestigious colleges like he had. He told me I wasn't polished enough. He told me the problem was I didn't have anything in common with them, so I didn't know what to say to them. He was right."

"Maybe you should have said, 'My husband's an idiot of the first degree and he's trying to make his shallowness all my fault.' If they weren't superficial assholes like him, then you'd probably have found plenty to talk about after that."

Rebecca laughed. "How do you do that?"

"What?"

"Make me feel better."

He crossed the room and sat on the edge of the bed so his hip was against her thigh. She was wearing more baggy clothes again, so all he could appreciate about her was that fair skin, rose mouth and big eyes that had compelled him to make promises he intended to keep for the rest of his life. "You're dangerous, lady," he said, shaking his head.

She laughed again. "You just want my cobbler."

He wanted more than that, he realized. He wanted her to be content. He wanted her to feel as if this marriage didn't drag her down the way her first one had. But he'd been the responsible type all his life. So that wasn't so strange, was it?

He'd married the woman so he wouldn't lose his child, but that didn't mean he couldn't care about the woman herself. If that meant letting her further into his life, letting her affect him and his routine a bit more, well, he wasn't going to mind it.

"Speaking of food," he said, keeping it casual, "we have a dinner tomorrow night. Does it count as my cooking night if I pick up the check?"

Her pretty eyes narrowed. "What kind of dinner?"

"A business dinner." He hadn't planned on taking her, to tell the truth, but he would have to include her in some of his social business occasions eventually. Marriage was going to affect him at least that much. And it would give him a chance to prove to her he was right about Dr. SOB being wrong about her. "But there will be other spouses there, and…well, you're mine."

"Am I?" Rebecca whispered.

"Yes." He leaned forward, despite those sharp knitting needles that were between them, because something said that the moment called for a kiss. That something was shouting at him, urging him to take her mouth and prove to her that he could make her feel better in lots of ways. That it wasn't a mistake to let each other get a little bit closer.

* * *

Rebecca shivered as she slid into the white and black satin dress. The June night was warm, but her hands were icy and there was a cold ball where her stomach was supposed to be. Maybe she should tell Trent she was ill and couldn't attend the business dinner with him.

He'd assume it was because of the pregnancy and she wouldn't have to tell him what was really making her sick—nerves.

She slid her palms down her thighs, and the light caught on the simple platinum band on her left hand. Nerves or not, she was married to him. That meant something to her—despite her bad first attempt at the institution and despite the particular circumstances of this try.

She owed it to Trent, to herself and to their baby, to give her best shot at doing right by him tonight.

Balancing against the dresser top with one hand, she slipped into the black patent-leather sandals she'd purchased that day. The clerk who'd helped her select the dress had specified nothing less than three-inch heels and a matching purse no larger than a three-by-five index card. A novice at this kind of shopping, she'd obeyed.

Now she took a deep breath and, closing her eyes, spun around to face the full-length mirror on the closet door. *Okay, Eisenhower, let's see if your mom can pull this off.*

Her stomach jittered as her lashes lifted. She swallowed hard. "Oh boy," she whispered. "Oh boy, oh boy, oh boy."

White satin strips covered her breasts but left enough

skin showing that she'd had to buy a special low-cut bra to wear under the dress. Beneath her breasts was a band of black satin, and then more white fell in an A-line to skim her knees. If there was any pregnancy change to her midriff, this dress didn't show it. The clerk had pointed out to an indecisive Rebecca that the garment wasn't skimpy or clingy, but now on a second look, she saw that the dress did nothing to hide the one area of her body that *had* begun to change.

She had cleavage. Honest-to-goodness cleavage.

She walked closer to the mirror, staring at herself, and the freshwater-pearl- and sterling-silver lariat necklace that she'd found on sale brushed the inside curves of her breasts. Her skin started to tingle.

The sensation reminded her of Trent, of Trent kissing her the night before, and the tingles raced over her again. It had been a brief kiss, but even the memory of it could melt the cold knot in her stomach.

What was he going to think about her now?

As if on cue, she heard his voice call up the stairs. "Rebecca? Are you about ready?"

She pressed her lips together to suppress a giddy giggle. She was ready. But was he? Maybe this time all the electrical jolts wouldn't be one-sided. Maybe now she'd send a bolt or two *his* way.

As she reached the top of the stairs, he glanced up. It was one of those moments that a woman waits a lifetime for.

His eyes widened. She saw his hand jerk up to catch hold of the newel. Her confidence soared.

"Hell," he said aloud. "Who are you?"

"That might be the nicest compliment I've ever had in my life." Oh, yes, she thought she *could* do right by him tonight.

He continued staring. "Your hair…"

It was down around her shoulders, side-parted, in loose ringlets.

His free hand made a vague gesture. "Your face…"

Maybe she needed to wear mascara more often. Tonight, she'd double-coated it, and selected a plum lipstick that was two shades darker than her usual color.

Then his gaze drifted down. His knuckles whitened on the newel. "Your—" Blinking, he caught himself. "Your, uh, *dress*. It's…it's…it's…"

Afraid he might say "overflowing," she took pity on him and started down the steps. "Yes, well, it kind of surprised me, too. Shall we go?"

At the bottom of the stairway he took her hand. "Must we?" he asked, his voice soft.

The tingles raced over her again, prickling her scalp, sliding beneath her dress, causing goose bumps to rise beneath the natural-colored stockings she wore. She looked at his mouth and remembered again how he'd kissed her the night before. His mouth had been firm, but restrained. She'd wanted to lean into it, lean into him, but just as she'd felt herself moving, he'd moved himself. Away, up, out the bedroom door.

Now his thumb stroked over her knuckles. "I know a place that can deliver an entire candlelight dinner in twenty minutes."

Her mouth went dry. "I thought this dinner was about business. *Your* business."

He blinked. "Business." Then he dropped her hand and rubbed his palm over his hair and across the back of his neck. "How could I forget business?"

Rebecca walked around him to pick up her tiny purse from the foyer table where she'd placed it. He wasn't looking at her.

"Business," she thought she heard him mutter again. "I never forget business."

Once in his car, he kept his gaze trained out the windshield. "So you know, there will be eight in our party at the club."

"The club?"

"The Tanglewood Country Club."

"Ah." Of course, the Tanglewood Country Club. She'd heard of it from her ex. He'd wanted to join for years, and had been seeking someone to sponsor him. Cold started to creep over her again.

"These are out-of-town clients whom I've only met a couple of times before myself. Stephanie Fox started her own Web-based, long-term data-storage company about five years back. She's here with her husband, and two people from her office, along with their respective spouses. We won't be talking business tonight, just getting better acquainted."

Great, Rebecca thought. And she was barely acquainted with her husband. "Do you…go to the country club often?"

"I'm the head of the membership committee and the president-elect."

"Well," she said, hearing her voice thin with nerves, "then I suppose you'll see a lot of familiar faces there tonight."

"Probably." He hesitated. "In preparation, I made a few calls today telling friends and family about our marriage."

"You did?"

"I didn't think it necessary to share all the details of our situation, so I said we'd been set up by a mutual friend and had a whirlwind courtship. The pregnancy announcement can come later, don't you think?"

"Oh, I hate the lies. Who's this mutual friend supposed to be?"

Trent's lips twitched. "Morgan Davis. So no lie, after all."

No lie. But their marriage was an even more concrete reality now that other people knew about it. And she'd promised herself to give it her best, even though she was a blue-collar navy brat paired with a CEO who also happened to be the president-elect of one of the most prestigious country clubs in the country. Dread grew inside her as he pulled into the club's parking lot. He surprised her by cruising past the waiting parking valet and finding his own spot in a secluded corner.

Then he turned off the ignition and shifted to face her. "The tension's coming off you in waves, Rebecca. Let's sit here a minute while you take a few deep breaths, okay?"

"You must think I'm foolish."

"I think you're naturally apprehensive over a new situation. But you'll be fine, I promise." He reached out, probably to pat her hands clenched around her tiny bag, but her jittery nerves had her jerking away.

The purse's latch scraped against her stockinged leg bared by the short dress, snagging the fine mesh. Immediately, an inch-wide run zipped toward her ankle. Rebecca stared down at it, aghast. "No! No, no, no, no, no. I can't go in like this!" She looked back up at Trent. "I *told* you I'd be a failure."

"Rebecca—" He stopped, laughed. "I've lived too long when I realize this isn't the moment for logic. So let's just solve the easiest problem, okay? Take 'em off."

"What? Take what off?"

"Take off the stockings, or the panty hose, whatever they are."

"I don't even want to walk into the country club with this ugly run!"

"Then take them off right here," he answered.

She sucked in a breath then heard herself grumble, "Have you forgotten this isn't the moment for logic?"

He laughed again. "If you can joke, you can divest yourself of some clothing."

"Oh, all right," she said. "Close your eyes."

"Why?"

"Because I have to lift up my skirt, that's why."

His eyebrows rose. "You're trying to get me to forget about business again, aren't you?"

And that had *her* laughing, and feeling attractive again. And confident. A few minutes later, as they approached the doors of the country club's restaurant, the breeze against her bare legs caused barely a shiver.

Once inside, Rebecca had a moment to take in the surroundings. It wasn't a large room, but it was filled with round tables covered with dark green linens. Ornamental grasses and bared, delicate branches made up unusual centerpieces. One entire wall was glass, affording a view of an Asian-inspired garden and waterfall. Men were wearing dark suits, and the women's throats and wrists glittered with rhinestones.

No, Rebecca realized. Diamonds. These women wore the real thing.

And she wasn't the real thing. Not a real wife to Trent Crosby. Not the *kind* of wife he would really choose for himself.

The thought hit her, hard, just as all the heads in the room seemed to turn their way. On stiff legs she managed to follow the maître d' to their table. As they passed, she heard people hail Trent, but she kept up her pace. Ahead, she could see more strangers grouped around a table with two empty places.

Their dinner companions. Trent's business dinner companions.

People she didn't know for dinner with a man she didn't know but had married.

This wasn't going to work, she thought again in a panic. *I won't have anything to say to these people, Eisenhower.* She was going to let Trent down. Then she felt his hand on the small of her back. His voice whispered in her ear. "Two men just begged me for your phone number. I had to disappoint them and say you were permanently taken."

Startled, she looked over her shoulder at him.

He shrugged. "It's those naked legs, honey. We're all at their mercy."

That word, *naked,* derailed her. Suddenly she was thinking of her naked legs, of Trent admiring them, and whether his comment was even true or not, she found herself sitting down, smiling, shaking hands as she met the people at their table.

It was like that for the rest of the evening. Every time she stumbled, every time those awkward doubts tried to overtake her, he was there, touching her hand, murmuring something into her ear, making her smile or laugh. Making her relax.

Ray had always left her alone at social gatherings with his friends. Sink or swim, he'd say. And she'd always felt she'd floundered.

As they pulled into the driveway at the end of the night, Trent told her to stay put and then came around to help her out of the car. Gently pulling her from her seat, he said, "You did it. You should feel proud of yourself."

"I was determined to do right by you," she said. He gave her a surprised glance, but didn't release her hand as he led her into the house. In the foyer, she tugged him to face her. "And I realize, Trent, I realize…"

He stepped closer, his thighs just inches from her naked ones. *Naked.*

"I realize…"

His free hand stroked down her cheek, then back up to tuck a curl behind her ear. "What do you realize?"

She couldn't catch her breath. His touch was putting that strange, sexual spell on her again, making her forget who she was, why she was here. *Naked.* She couldn't seem to get that word out of her head.

"I realize that instead, Trent, you did right by me."

"'Did' right by you?" He smiled and in the dim light it flashed with the same bright whiteness of his shirt. "Darling, I haven't even gotten started doing right by you."

His head dipped down.

Trent let his mouth hover over Rebecca's. He needed a moment before she knocked him on his ass again. Because surely she would.

Every time he thought he had a handle on their situation, she shook things up again. Called their marriage a mistake. Drew up household schedules. Informed him she'd wanted to "do right" by him.

Appeared at the top of the stairs tonight like something out of a dream.

His lips landed hard on hers. She tasted like warmth and surprise and there was that pillowy bottom lip that made him think of long, lazy afternoons. He swiped his tongue against it.

She shivered, and he cupped her shoulders in his palms. His mouth moved across her cheek and she moaned in his ear as he moved down the creamy flesh of her neck. "Your legs weren't the only things making me crazy all night," he murmured against her throat.

Her breasts. There should be odes written to those breasts. They were creamy, like the rest of her skin, and plump. Man, they were plump. He backed off a little and let his forefinger wander down the neckline of her dress. Under his other hand, he felt her quiver again.

"Rebecca."

She was staring down at his hand, fascinated, it seemed, by the slow, tracing movement of his darker-skinned finger along her fine-pored flesh.

"Rebecca, we need to talk."

Her head came up. "About what?"

"About..." The answer was simple, wasn't it? There was no sense denying themselves any longer. It was time they took this to his bedroom and did something with all the sexual heat simmering between them. Wouldn't it only cement their partnership? Then she'd never bring up that mistake business again.

Beneath his stroking fingertip, he felt her skin heat. He drew his knuckle upward again, painting a slow line toward the thrumming pulse in her neck. Maybe they shouldn't talk at all. He was rock-hard, she was trembling, and words could get in the way.

Leaning down, he captured her mouth again. He slid his tongue inside and felt her little hum of response. She stumbled closer, and he slid his hands down to her hips and tilted hers against his own. That hum reverberated through the both of them this time.

Her mouth tore free of his and she stared in the direction of his pants. "Wh-what's happening?"

He gazed down at her, half-dazed himself. "You're a nurse, you figure it out."

Then he felt that little buzz again, only it didn't come from her. It came from him. His pants. With a groan, he shoved his hand in his front pocket and pulled out a cell phone. "What the hell? I grabbed this before we left, but this isn't mine." And he never put his on vibrate.

Rebecca swiped it out of his hand. "It's mine." She frowned at the screen, then flipped the phone open and brought it to her ear. "The hospital," she said to him, then into the phone, "This is Rebecca."

In an instant her demeanor changed. She went from dreamy female to hyper-alert nurse. "When? How long? I will, right away." With a *clack,* she snapped the phone shut.

"What is it? What's the problem?"

"Merry." She was already rushing for the door. "Her asthma's acting up again. They've admitted her and she's calling for me."

"I'll drive you."

She skidded to a halt. "No. Oh, no. I'm sorry, I—" Her cheeks flushed pink. "This was your business evening and…"

And they'd been heading for a lusty workout on his mattress upstairs. "And while I'd like to stomp my feet and then pout in the corner over the change of plans, my car is blocking yours and I'd feel better about driving you than having you drive yourself over there at this time of night."

"It's nothing new."

"Being married to me is." He didn't let her protest further. The fact was, he *did* want to stomp his feet and pout, but she'd said the magic word. *Merry.* He remembered the little girl. He and Rebecca could postpone their date between the sheets for an hour or so until the child settled down for the night.

The hour or so turned into four.

It was the wee hours of the morning when he heard her dismayed voice. "Trent! I thought I told someone to make you go home."

He removed the tattered *People* magazine he'd splayed over his face and sat up on his mattress of four molded plastic chairs. "A beefy, fifty-something orderly came by and told me I wasn't good enough for you, if that's what you mean."

"Oh." She pulled around her the ends of the lab coat she wore over her dress and dropped onto one of the seats beside him. "Sorry about that. I had to explain about you. People here know you're my husband now."

Husband. Rebecca's husband.

Now he understood why she'd looked so odd when he'd told her he'd informed friends and family of their marriage. It felt different to know Rebecca's friends were looking at him, judging him. Their relationship didn't seem so simple, so straightforward any longer. "A woman whose badge read Peggy brought me a Danish. Does that mean she approves of me?"

Rebecca closed her eyes and rested her head against the back of her chair. "If you have a Y chromosome, Peggy approves of you."

"Oh." He should have known it wouldn't be that easy. "How's Merry?"

"Sleeping now. It's been a rough few hours for her."

Trent noted the new paleness of Rebecca's face. "For you, too."

She rolled her head from side to side to ease the stiffness in her neck. "It's the light in here. Makes everyone pasty."

He stood up, then grabbed her hands and pulled her to her feet. "Upsy-daisy, pasty lady. Time for bed."

Her gaze flew to his. Messages flew back and forth.

We almost made it there tonight, together.

Yes.

Do you feel relief or regret?

Yes.

Looking at the exhausted woman in front of him, Trent realized that going to bed with Rebecca was a lot more serious than the simple slaking of lust that he'd had in mind. Cementing their partnership with sex had repercussions he hadn't let himself consider. Here was a woman who cared about people, who cared *for* people as her profession.

She made apple cobbler, for God's sake.

This was a woman unlike his selfish mother or his self-absorbed first wife. She wasn't a one-night stand, either. He could do damage here if he didn't tread very, very carefully.

"Let's go home, Rebecca." He'd never thought of it as that, as "home," but now he discovered there might be something new to the word.

Just like simple wasn't so simple anymore. But he was still right—she'd found a way to knock him on his ass once more.

Seven

Three days later, Trent arrived home in the late afternoon. He slammed shut the front door, dumped his briefcase on the foyer table and scowled at the neat pile of mail. The scent of something sugary beckoned from the kitchen, but it didn't sweeten his lousy mood.

"Trent, is that you?" Rebecca's voice called from the direction of the den.

"Yeah." He didn't dare go near her.

At the moment, women were dangerous to him. Tall, short, young, old, the entire female half of the world was out to drive him nuts.

"Trent, is everything all right?" The gentle note of concern only served to rub him wrong.

"No, everything is very *not* all right," he muttered.

"What?"

I'm a man. You're a woman. Let's have sex. But he couldn't lead with that, could he?

"My own assistant just kicked me out of the building," he yelled in frustration instead. "My littler sister apparently considers herself the queen of my life as well as the Queen of Lantanya, because she called four times this morning to berate me about keeping quiet about our wedding. My other sister is insisting on hosting a reception for us, and when I told her where she could stuff her ideas for a cake, she cried. Cried, damn it! That got *her* assistant ticked at me. So I go to their offices to apologize—though why I should, I don't know—and apparently I shoved open the door, startling the assistant who was conducting an emergency trim on her teenage daughter's bangs. I've been informed the bangs suffered. *That* got the fourteen-year-old crying, and moments later there was a corridor full of women who were staring at me as if I'd personally ordered the cancellations of both Oprah's and Dr. Phil's talk shows. And they claim *I've* been in a bad mood lately!"

He paused to take a breath.

He *had* been in a bad mood lately. A hell of a frustrated mood.

"And it's all your fault," he muttered.

"What was that last part?"

He strode toward the den, determined to get this out in the open. Living with Rebecca and not being able to touch her was turning his mood nastier by the day. He'd held off coaxing her into bed because he was afraid of hurting her, but the one who was hurting was him.

And everyone he came in contact with.

"Look, Rebecca, I'm a man. And you're a woman." A woman who had brought her woman's scents into his house, who had brought fantasies of her womanly body—her legs, her breasts, her smooth, pale skin—into his head. "Don't you think it's time we—"

He halted in the doorway, staring at what was in his den instead of Rebecca. The furniture was pushed against the walls. A box cutter and a full roll of packing tape lay on the carpet between himself and an edifice of heavy cardboard. "Rebecca?"

The edifice swayed, and a head half peeked out of a square cut into the side of one wall. "Yes?"

"Your playhouse," he guessed.

"*Merry's* playhouse. She's still in the hospital and I thought that when I go back on shift tomorrow I'd like to tell her I made some progress."

"A lot of progress."

The head disappeared and he heard the distinctive screech of sticky tape being stretched from a dispenser. "I'm taping down the interior walls." The playhouse swayed again and he heard another screech. "Now, what was it you were saying?"

He shook his head, trying to regain his thoughts. In a corner of the room, the television was alive and on it—wouldn't you know—was that smug Dr. Phil. Well, the guru would approve of his honesty, wouldn't he? "You're a woman, and I'm a m—"

"Would you mind holding this?"

"What?"

Her hand wiggled outside the window opening. "Just hold right here while I reinforce the edges, okay?"

He frowned. "Why don't we just buy Merry a playhouse?"

There was a tiny pause that made him feel like a bigfooted clod. "It wouldn't be the same."

Of course it wouldn't be the same. Before he made another female in his world cry, he crossed to the little window. Rebecca wanted him to hold some cardboard mullions in place, which required him to hunker down on the floor.

"Now," she said, over the screeching tape, "what is it you were telling me?"

He peered through the window. Rebecca must have been on her knees, too, because he could only see her between the neck and waist. She was wearing an old cutoff T-shirt—was it one of his?—and the knowledge of what was beneath it, what was distinctly hers, smooth and warm, started itching at him again.

I'm a man. You're a woman. Let's have sex.

It was as primal, as essential as that.

He could see it now. The two of them, tangled on his bed. Hell, tangled on the floor, right here, right now, that T-shirt pushed away, the sweatpants she was wearing pushed down and his mouth on her. Everywhere.

Dampness gathered along his spine. He sucked in a breath and drew her light perfume into his lungs. Powdery, sweet, womanly.

He shifted, trying to ease the pull of his slacks. He couldn't turn his gaze away from her shirt, as if any second, X-ray vision would melt the barrier between them.

He didn't want any more barriers. Of any kind.

She froze. Maybe his lust was that loud.

"Trent?"

"What?" His voice was hoarse. *I'm a man. You're a woman. Let's have sex.*

"Is something bothering you?"

Yes! Hell, yes! It was the perfect lead-in. He opened his mouth.

She moved, leaning sideways. The action lifted her T-shirt.

He saw it. Between the hem of the rising T-shirt and the waistband of the sweatpants was Rebecca's belly. Pale and smooth like her breasts. Warm and fragrant, he was sure, like all the rest of her skin.

The hairs on the back of his neck prickled. Under all that smooth, fragrant, Rebecca-skin, his child was growing.

The prickles rose all over his body. There was a baby, he'd been aware of that. His baby. He'd been aware of that, too. But until this second, he'd separated that from Rebecca. Somehow there'd been the woman, and then the child. He'd not seen her as a mother, *the* mother of *his* child.

Lust was replaced by reverence.

He rose, and then backed away from the playhouse, needing air, time, distance.

Man, woman, mother, child. Father.

And…fear.

It was as primal, as essential as that.

Rebecca returned to work and for a few days her life with Trent settled into a routine. Not the kind of marriage routine she'd envisioned with her shared-chores, shared-meals plan, but the kind of roommates' routine that she began to believe was what he'd had in mind from the beginning.

Perhaps those moments of sexual awareness had been something only she experienced, and those kisses he'd instigated only experiments.

Experiments that had failed, since he'd never gotten close enough for another.

"Doing okay?"

Her head jerked toward the kitchen entry. Trent stood there, his hair damp, his feet bare, wearing his suit trousers and his tieless, untucked dress shirt. It was his pre-coffee uniform.

"Doing okay?" he asked again.

It was his pre-coffee question. His home-from-work question. His just-passing-her-on-the-stairs/hall/front-porch question.

She smiled as she poured him a cup of coffee. "Doing fine." Her standard response.

He took the mug with a nod of thanks and stood beside her to drink it. Closing his eyes, he slowly drained the liquid.

She closed her eyes, too and drank in the scent of his just-showered self. The tangy, fresh smell of him woke her nerve endings better than caffeine ever had. His mug clacked against the countertop, and opening her eyes, she moved away from him.

He poured himself another full cup and she bustled about to brew her own small pot of green tea. "Busy day ahead?" she asked.

"Mmm."

She slid him a sidelong glance. He appeared preoccupied already, his gaze trained on his coffee. That was routine now, too—that he rarely looked at her. But it freed her to appreciate his handsomeness, a little pleasure that she indulged in without too much guilt. What woman wouldn't admire that strong, tall body and handsome features that belonged to the man she called husband?

In name only.

With a mental shrug, she pushed the small regret away. She'd wanted to make the best of their situation, to do the right thing by Trent and to do the right thing for Eisenhower. That had been accomplished.

She was satisfied.

Trent started out of the kitchen, mug in hand. She allowed herself to watch him leave, her gaze moving from the square cut of the hair at his nape to the muscular male curve of his behind.

Looking was enough.

At the doorway, he hesitated, then swung around.

She jerked up her gaze and felt herself flush. Had he felt her staring?

"It's wrong," he said.

Her eyes widened. "I…uh…" Should she apologize?

He ignored her stuttering. "It's wrong, but my sister Katie isn't going to let up until I—we give in."

Oh. Whew. He wasn't talking about the way she was getting her secret jollies. She swallowed. "Give in to what?"

"Dinner. Her house. Tonight."

"Tonight?" Rebecca's voice squeaked. "But...but..."

"Do it for me, Rebecca, will you? I should have told you days ago, but I kept thinking I'd come up with a way to talk her out of it."

"But..." The obvious presented itself first. "I don't have anything to wear."

"Not that black-and-white dress," he said instantly. "Please."

Rebecca's face burned. "Okay." She'd thought he'd liked it.

"My sister's a romantic."

What did that mean? What did that have to do with the black-and-white dress? She didn't know the man she'd married well enough to ask. She wondered if she ever would.

"My sister will want to see for herself that we're, uh, happy, even though I've assured her a dozen times." His eyes met hers. "And we are, Rebecca, right?"

"Sure." She'd just told herself she was satisfied. But would Trent's sister feel the same when she had a chance to judge her brother's marriage for herself?

Trent took Rebecca's hand as they ascended the steps to the wood-and-glass house—it looked like a mansion to Rebecca—that belonged to his sister Katie and her husband, Peter Logan. "Your fingers are cold," he said, tightening his grip. "You don't need to be nervous."

"Oh, I'm not. Traipsing into the home of wealthy strangers and playing an ecstatic, yet secretive newlywed comes natural to me."

"Rebecca." He stopped midway up the stairs. "Shall we leave? I can call and give her an excuse. She probably half expects it."

"I don't know. I don't know if I can do this, Trent." Her nerves had been jangling all day and the sight of the Logans' huge, sleek-looking house wasn't soothing them any. "She probably thinks I'm a gold digger."

"I already married one of those. Katie knows I don't make the same mistake twice."

"But what if we've both gotten this all wrong? You said your sister is a romantic. What if we're wrong about romance, about love, and we shouldn't have let our pessimism push us into this marriage?"

He half smiled. "Pessimism didn't push us into this marriage. An accident did. An accidental pregnancy."

"It wasn't an accident to me," she responded fiercely. "I *wanted* this baby."

His expression softened and he lifted his hand to caress her cheek. "What about this explanation, then? Maybe this…situation is destiny. Have you ever considered that? Maybe our marriage is fate."

She had a feeling he was humoring her. But it sounded better than a marriage made out of pessimism and a situation that came about through something as simple as human error. "Fate," she echoed. You could tell your grandchildren about fate.

Your granddad and I were destined to be together.
Were they?

She looked into Trent's eyes. "Do you think…?"

"I think…" He glanced toward the house. "I think we should leave. I'll tell Katie something came up."

"Oh, good. It's—" Rebecca began.

Ahead of them, the front door popped open and a young woman popped out her head. "Finally! You're here!"

Trent and Rebecca looked at each other and half smiled. "Too late," they said together.

Katie Crosby was close to Rebecca's age and radiant with pregnancy and happiness. Her brown hair was worn in a short, wispy style that made her dark eyes stand out. She wore a poppy-colored knit dress that showed off her six-months-along belly, the belly that she patted as she linked arms with Rebecca and drew her into the house.

"This place still feels a little cavernous to me, but neither Peter's loft nor my condo was big enough for the three of us. Did my brother prepare you with the news you'll be an aunt soon?" Katie threw a smile at Trent over her shoulder. "He keeps asking me when I'm going to start wearing maternity clothes, but I wore a baggy wardrobe for a lifetime, so as long as the spandex will stretch, I'm showing off all my curves."

A dark-haired man approaching them smiled and

held out his hand. "Peter Logan, curvy lady's husband. It's nice to meet you." He reached again to share another firm handshake with Trent.

"Come into the living room," Katie said. "Peter's parents happened to drop by for a drink."

Rebecca knew Terrence and Leslie Logan by sight. The older couple were legends around Portland General for their very generous contributions to Children's Connection as well as to the hospital itself. She shook hands with them, and even though she'd never dealt with them professionally and felt they were socially out of her reach, they put her at ease with their seemingly genuine interest in her position as an OR pediatric nurse.

"We didn't know you'd married, Trent," Leslie said, smiling. An attractive woman of around sixty, she seemed delighted to hear the news. "Please accept our congratulations."

Trent returned her smile. "Thank you, Leslie, I appreciate that."

Peter came by with a round of drinks, and beneath the clinking of ice and glasses, Rebecca heard her speak to Trent again, her voice soft. "And Danny, Trent. Katie says she hasn't talked to your brother recently, but that you have. How is Danny doing?"

Trent took a swallow from his glass. "The same, I guess. Okay."

"Tell him I asked after him. Please," the older woman said.

"I will." Trent's nod was stiff.

Danny was the brother whose son had been kidnapped. The one who'd been friends with the Logans' little boy, Robbie, who'd suffered the same fate. Rebecca felt a chill run down her back, and she crossed to stand beside Trent. He put his arm around her.

Maybe it was just an act for his sister, but she appreciated the gesture all the same.

"Sit down, everyone," Katie said. "I'm going to put up my swollen feet and Peter is going to serve the hors d'oeuvres, won't you, honey?"

The serious expression on her husband's face vanished at that "honey." He gave her a smile that tugged at Rebecca's heart. "Only if you let me rub those feet later."

Katie's face turned pink. "Peter!"

He grinned and mimicked her embarrassed exclamation. "Katie! Considering the state of your belly, my darling, I'm sure even your big brother here realizes you've let me touch you a time or two."

The others in the room laughed, though Katie turned even redder and rolled her eyes. "Men!" she said, then dropped onto the couch and patted the place beside her. "Come sit next to me, Rebecca, and you and Leslie and I can commiserate."

Terrence Logan sent both his wife and Katie a fond smile. "Sorry, daughter-in-law, but we can't stay long. We're here to tell Peter what we learned at the Children's Connection directors' meeting." He glanced at Rebecca. "It's something of a family endeavor, you see, supporting the place."

"We can go to my study, Dad," Peter started.

"No," Leslie interrupted. "We're all family here. As a matter of fact, Trent himself helped out a few months back, though I'm not sure he knew why Morgan and the Children's Connection lawyer, Justin Weber, asked him for that favor."

Katie shot her brother a glance. "What favor?"

He replied with one word, tersely stated. "Mom."

"Mom?" Katie echoed. "What now?"

He hesitated, his gaze darting around the room and then landing on Rebecca's face. "Katie…"

"You haven't warned her about Mom?" Katie asked, shaking her head. "Then let me fill her in. It was our mother who should have been watching our brother Danny and Robbie Logan the day he was kidnapped. But she was her usual neglectful self and we've all paid for it."

"Katie." Trent's voice was a warning.

His sister flashed him a look. "Don't bother denying it. You blamed yourself, Leslie blamed herself, our fathers feuded, our companies became bitter rivals, not to mention what Danny went through then and again when he lost Noah and after that, Felicia. It's a miracle that Peter and I managed to find each other through all that pain!"

Peter perched on the edge of the couch and stroked his wife's hair. "Katie. Sweetheart."

"Well, I'm right, aren't I?" Katie switched her gaze to him. "If it wasn't for fate—"

"I thought that was me," Peter put in with a little smile, "tracking you down in Wyoming."

Fate, Rebecca thought. It was sounding better all the time.

"Fate and your persistence, then," Katie amended. "But my mother still tries to turn all the past tragedies around and make *herself* victim!"

Peter stroked her hair again. "It's not good for the baby if you get so worked up."

"And it's not good for Rebecca to be unaware of the true colors of her mother-in-law, either." She ran a hand over her belly and looked back at Trent. "So what has she been up to?"

He shrugged. "Beats me. I only know that Morgan and Justin called and requested a favor. They asked if I would apply some pressure on Mom about her country-club membership—tell her that if she started spreading rumors about Children's Connection that I would revoke her privileges at Tanglewood. I didn't ask any more questions of them, and the minute I broached the subject, Mom saw the writing on the wall and clammed up."

All eyes in the room turned to Terrence. He cleared his throat. "Let me start from the beginning. You're all aware of the Sanders baby being found?"

"We saw it in the papers and on the news, Dad," Peter said, "but there were very few details given."

And not any more from the PAN meeting she'd attended, Rebecca remembered, or via the hospital grapevine in the days afterward, which was even more surprising.

"There's more to the story, much more. It has all

been part of an elaborate scheme that's purportedly about money, but that seems to me to be about discrediting Children's Connection as well. First, there was a heist of frozen eggs from our Portland clinic that were subsequently put up for sale on an illegal Internet site. Then, babies intended for adoption here in the U.S. through our Russian affiliate were stolen and then sold on the black market, though thank God the FBI was able to put a stop to that and apprehend the man on the Russian end. There was the Sanders baby, as I said—"

"And what about what happened to my sister, Ivy?" Katie interjected, then looked over at Rebecca. "Months ago someone tried to steal the baby she was holding as part of the baby rockers program for the drug-addicted infants."

Rebecca nodded. She remembered the incident well.

"That assault on Ivy was part of it, too," Terrence confirmed. "Part of another plan, a plan to steal American babies from impoverished mothers and then sell them to wealthy families who want quick, no-questions-asked adoptions."

Peter shook his head, then sighed. "Who would do such a thing?"

"And why do you think it wasn't purely about the money?" Trent added.

Terrence shrugged. "Just a hunch I have at this point."

The room was silent a moment, then Peter spoke up again. "Okay, Dad, so how do we know all this?"

"Because a young man came forward in the last few

days and confessed his involvement to the authorities who'd been looking for him, though they've been trying to keep it out of the press. It was he who let them know where the Sanders baby could be found. His name is Everett Baker."

"Everett Baker!" Rebecca exclaimed.

Now those in the room gave *her* their attention, and she felt herself flush. "Not that I know him, not really. But he's an accountant at Children's Connection, isn't that right?"

"He was," Terrence said. "How did you know?"

"Because I know Nancy Allen—another one of the nurses at Portland General. Everyone knows Nancy. She's one of those warm souls who talks to everyone and everyone talks to her. No one has said that she had anything to do with this?"

Terrence shook his head. "I haven't heard that she did."

Rebecca frowned. "I wouldn't believe it. Nancy is wonderful. She has a heart a mile wide and an affinity for picking up strays. I saw her talking to Everett in the cafeteria a few times and that's where I met him—with her." In her mind, she pictured the tall, lean man who rarely smiled, unless it was at Nancy. "I was sure there was a romance developing between the two of them."

"And so another heart gets broken," Trent murmured.

Terrence's eyebrows rose. "I wouldn't be so sure. What I *have* been told is that this nurse is standing by Everett and that he listed her as one of the reasons he finally came clean."

Leslie Logan looked at her husband. "If this woman is as wonderful as Rebecca says, and she sees something worthwhile in Everett Baker, then maybe there's hope for him."

Peter gave his mother a fond smile. "The eternal optimist, aren't you, Mom?"

"I saw you through puberty, didn't I?"

They all laughed again, but then Katie frowned. "Wait a second. I'm not seeing our mother's link to Children's Connection."

"Oh. Well." Terrence cleared his throat again and his gaze dropped. "She, uh, happened to have come across some information about what was happening that she could have used to make Children's Connection look incompetent."

"Come across, how?" Katie persisted.

"How do you think?" Trent asked, a sour note in his voice. "Pillow talk, I presume?"

Terrence nodded. "One of our directors happened to tell your mother about yet another 'mishap' involving the clinic. I don't know any of the people involved, and I trust that all of you will keep this to yourselves, but there was a problem with a couple of inseminations and the sperm used."

Rebecca felt herself go still. She didn't dare look at Trent.

"They thought the first instance was an accident," the older man said. "But went ahead and rechecked all the recent procedures. When they found another insemination and subsequent pregnancy from the wrong sperm, the clinic took a long hard look at the circumstances and possibilities. They were coming to the conclusion that these mix-ups weren't mix-ups, after all, when Everett's confession confirmed what they suspected. The sperm mix-ups weren't accidents. And not mistakes, either. They were—"

"Malicious," Rebecca finished. She couldn't help herself. And now she couldn't help looking at Trent. They weren't together due to an accident or to simple human error.

And not because of fate either.

Eight

After the dinner at Katie and Peter's, Trent took Rebecca home and then steered her into the kitchen. She'd appeared somewhat relaxed and animated at his sister's, but she'd gone tense and quiet in the car on the way back. He pushed her into a chair, raided the cookie jar for a handful of cookies that he put on a plate in front of her. Then he inspected the fridge, bypassing the pitcher of green tea to pour them both some lemonade.

He took a seat across from her and pushed a glass her way. "All right, out with it." He wouldn't sleep until he silenced all the voices that he could tell were whirling in Rebecca's brain.

She sighed. "Tonight…"

"Was a success. My sister thinks you're great. Peter

got to drill you on baby stuff." Trent shook his head. "There's an overprotective father in the making."

She went silent again, staring down at the table. "It's not fair to you," she finally said.

He took a swallow from his glass, eyeing her over the rim. "About Peter? Don't see how. I'll probably be an overprotective dad myself."

"It's not fair to you that you're going to be a father."

She was going to bring up that mistake business again. He frowned.

"You didn't want a child right now," she continued. "I did."

"So—"

"So it wasn't anything as…magical, as spiritual as fate that made me pregnant with your baby. It was someone's ugly, malicious act!"

Trent stilled. He could point out that the end result was the same, that if she was going to have his child— by whatever means it had happened—he was deter- mined to be the baby's father. He could bring fate back into the picture again by mentioning that some Greater Order had certainly still had its hand in. Of all the vials that had been rearranged, it was Trent's, after all, that had found its way to Rebecca. But that wouldn't cheer her either.

"Something 'ugly' is not part of our baby, Rebecca."

"I don't want it to be," she whispered. "I wish it wasn't."

He reached across for her hand. "Nothing that has to do with you could ever be ugly." After averting his gaze from her for days, he hadn't been able to avoid looking at her that evening. She wore a matching skirt and sweater, both in a soft fabric the color of vanilla ice cream. Her hair was down in those loose, sexy curls again. "I couldn't keep my eyes off you all night."

She darted him a swift look. "Thanks."

But no cigar. She wasn't fishing for compliments. "What do you need, Rebecca? Can you tell me that?"

"You didn't want a child," she said again. "You didn't want a wife."

"I want you."

Those Bambi eyes met his for another instant, dropped again. "Right."

"Every day, Rebecca. Every night."

She shook her head. "You don't need to say that."

But he needed to *do* something. That was clear. And what he needed to do and what he wanted to do were suddenly coming together in one idea that felt entirely right to him. "Tell me about the insemination procedure, Rebecca."

Her gaze flew to his and her eyes flared wide. *"What?"*

"Well, I'm assuming there's a room, a table, and some kind of turkey baster, right?"

"Trent!" Her cheeks flushed red.

"No soft music, no candlelight, no kisses and caresses, I presume."

She frowned at him. "Of course not. Though I think I remember humming 'Yankee Doodle Dandy' while I was waiting for the doctor to come in."

He stood, pulling her up with him. "Hum it for me now, sweetheart, and we'll dance."

She went stiff as he pulled her against him. "What are you doing?"

Since she seemed unwilling to cooperate, he started humming himself, an old Beatles tune, "Eleanor Rigby." So it wasn't a love song, but he knew how it went and it was getting her moving about the kitchen with him. He danced her over to the light switch and flicked it off.

They fox-trotted through the dining room, through the foyer, where he danced her in circles at the bottom of the stairs. He figured she only went along with it because she was relieved they'd moved away from the intimate and embarrassing discussion of insemination.

His cheek rubbed against the top of her head and he breathed her in, all that sweetness that had been filling his house and his thoughts, everything down to the damn pillows on his bed, which he wished she'd been sharing with him. He let his lips drift over her temple, then down her cheek, then back up to her ear. "Rebecca, let's make a baby tonight," he whispered.

She tried to go stiff on him again, but he sent soothing hands down her back to her curvy hips and then back up again. "Shh," he said. "Take it easy."

"Trent—"

"I know what you're thinking. Besides what a gorgeous hunk of man I am, of course. You're thinking that there already is a baby. But *we* didn't get to do that together. That was between you and the turkey baster and I have to confess I'm feeling a little bit neglected."

He felt a laugh bubble out of her and figured all those damn hours he'd spent at cotillions as a kid, learning to dance, were finally paying off.

"I wish you'd shut up about that turkey baster," she complained.

"Then give me something else to think about." He moved his lips to touch the corner of her mouth. The real plan was to give *her* something else to think about besides those voices and doubts, those fears and worries that were tumbling around in her head. For his part, there was little going on inside of him now but lust and the lingering smoke of his own brilliance.

Take her to bed and take the doubts away. Give her something else to think about and give you both a shared memory of making your baby.

He moved his lips the last millimeter to cover hers. She jerked in his arms, but he held her steady against his body and helped himself to the taste of her mouth.

She moaned, a good sign.

Then the tip of her tongue reached out to meet his, and the brief touch burned like lightning down his body. He deepened the kiss, pressing into her mouth so that he could feel it surround him. She snuggled closer and the combination went to his head—that wet, carnal kiss and that cuddly, curly-headed valentine against his heart.

He tore his mouth from hers and started leading her up the stairs.

"No more dancing?" she asked. Her eyes were smoky dark and her mouth already looked swollen. He thought he'd extinguished the last of her resistance.

"I could try to Astaire you up the steps, sweetheart, but I'm afraid finesse is out of my range at the moment. The only part of my body that's ready for any tricky movement is a part that doesn't dance."

They'd reached the landing and he paused to take her into his arms again. This kiss was hotter than the first one, and the night suddenly felt like August, not June. Without lifting his mouth, he yanked at his tie even as he shrugged out of his suit jacket.

He knew he'd extinguished the last of her resistance when she pulled the tails of his shirt from his pants and then ran her hands along his bare back.

Lightning burned him again at the touch. Needing air, he turned his head so he could breathe and taste the skin of her cheek at the same time.

She shivered. "I think—"

"I don't want you to think." He bit her ear and she trembled against him. He slid his hands down to her cute round butt and scrunched the material of her skirt in his fists so he could find her panties and then slide his fingers beneath them. He moved his mouth back to hers. "Thinking now?" he said.

She tipped her head back and tilted her hips into his. "Maybe a little," she whispered.

He swooped down for a deep, dark kiss, kneading her soft flesh in his hands as he explored her mouth. Desperate for breath, he pulled away and looked down into her half-closed eyes. "What's the capital of Rhode Island?"

She didn't even blink. "Providence."

He frowned. "Damn it, woman. Don't tell me I'm losing my touch."

She let him pull her up the next flight of stairs. "I'm sorry. I memorized them in eighth grade for extra credit and they've never gone away."

At the top of the steps he paused again. This time he slid his hands beneath the hem of her top, taking it away in one smooth action that bared a satin bra and that abundance of pale breasts that he'd gone gaga over the night of the country-club dinner. "Rebecca." He stroked his palms over her shoulders then over her breasts, cupping them in his hands. His thumbs met at her breastbone and he could feel her heart racing.

He kissed her again, then dropped down a step so that he had better access to that glorious cleavage. Her skin was hot against his tongue and he ran it all along the edges of the bra. She stroked his hair and her fast breaths lifted her flesh to his mouth. Through the satin fabric, he captured one nipple. Sucked.

Her fingernails bit into his scalp and she bowed against him.

Need ran down his spine and up from his toes. "Rebecca, what's the capital of West Virginia?"

Her voice was thready and sounded dazed. "Richmond?"

He clucked his tongue, then swiped it over the plump top curve of her breasts. "No, honey."

"Arlington?"

He shook his head as he ran his hands up her bare

legs—man, she had awesome legs!—to find her panties again. "Are you confused?"

"No, I—" She gasped as he yanked her underwear to her ankles. "I—"

"Lift up, honey," he said, patting one foot. She complied and he pulled her panties free first from one foot, and then the other.

"Charleston!" she suddenly said. "Charleston, *West* Virginia."

He looked up and shook his head. "You are entirely too focused, Nurse Rebecca. You're forcing me to bring out the big guns."

Hooking a finger around one of his belt loops, she tugged him up the step. A tiny, wicked smile played at the corners of her mouth as she went to work on the buckle. "The big guns? Oh, please," she said. "Let me."

His heart slammed against his chest. His erection stiffened to full salute. His valentine, he realized, had gone from soft pink to red hot.

She got him naked, and damn if she still didn't remember the capital of Arkansas. At least he thought she got it right; he couldn't be sure, because his brain was starting to steam around the edges. So then he lifted her in his arms and took the lesson into the bedroom and to his bed.

With his finger, he drew a map of Oregon on her naked midriff and made her name the points of interest that he kissed. She quivered a bit when he touched his tongue to Crater Lake, but got them all right.

She proved her knowledge of the geography of his

chest by tracing the muscles there with her fingers and then with her tongue.

He finally surrendered to temptation and took off her bra. Instead of teasing her with another question, he teased her breasts, tracing elaborate geometric figures on each plump form but studiously avoiding the sensitive centers. When her hips were twisting in his hands, he put his mouth over one nipple and drew in deeply.

She cried out, so needy that he realized she was balancing on the very edge.

"Oh, Rebecca," he said, staring down at her flushed cheeks and disheveled hair. Her mouth was wet, her nipple was wet. When he ran his hand beneath her skirt, she was wet there, too.

She jerked into his light touch. "Trent, please."

He slid her skirt off her body, then pressed one finger inside her and lost his breath as her muscles tightened on him. "Rebecca, you feel so good."

"*You* feel so good."

"No, you," he teased, pulling out and pressing in again.

She gasped, and one of her hands clutched his forearm. "Trent, I—"

"Go ahead," he said, "I'll take care of you." She wasn't thinking at all now, he decided with smug satisfaction. She was pure sensation.

Then her eyes popped open, proving him wrong once again. "No, Trent. With me. We—we need to make our baby."

His own idea startled him. Shocked him with the visceral, visual punch it made. "Rebecca," he murmured, then leaned down to kiss her, to move into her mouth as his hand moved out of her body and he positioned himself between her legs.

She made room for him instantly, widening her thighs so that their satiny warmth rubbed against his hips. That alone almost set him off.

He lifted his head so he could watch himself breach the opening to her body. Her breath hitched as he pushed in, and he glanced up to see her watching, too. "It's beautiful, isn't it?" he murmured. "This making-babies business is beautiful."

Her eyes closed as he sank in to the hilt. He lowered his chest so that it brushed the hard tips of her breasts, and they rocked together, once, twice, three times.

The rhythm caught, and he felt her passion rising again.

"Beautiful," she whispered.

At the word, the climax caught him. He pumped into it, feeling her body gather, then still, then shake with pleasure. He poured himself into her, letting go in bursts of passion that wrung him out. When it was over, he rested against the pillow of her breasts.

She was wrung out, too. When he rolled off her, she was a rag doll that he was able to gather into his arms and hold against his body as she drifted into sleep.

While he thought.

Before, sex had always been a mind-numbing ride, but now his mind wouldn't shut down. They'd made a baby. They had a baby. He cupped his palm against Rebecca's belly and imagined the life growing beneath his hand.

It didn't scare him anymore.

But the woman in his arms— Oh God, she did.

Because he had a bad feeling that if anyone could, Rebecca could make him want to believe again.

It seemed fitting that the first person to greet Rebecca the next morning was her ex. At dawn, she'd slipped out of Trent's bed—he hadn't stirred—and slipped out of the house as quickly as possible. Her shift at the hospital started at 6:00 a.m. that day and she'd decided to get her tea in the hospital cafeteria.

That was where Ray found her. He came up behind her in the checkout line, carrying a tall coffee and smelling of the overpriced cologne he'd asked for and she'd bought him four Christmases before. "If it isn't the beautiful bride!"

When she turned to reply, he actually took a step back. "What is it, Ray?" she asked. "Am I not so beautiful, after all?"

He frowned. "No, I…"

With a shake of her head, she faced forward again. "Becca."

She didn't look at him. "What is it, Ray?"

"You *are* beautiful. I'd forgotten."

Right. "What do you want? I found your old baseball cards and gave them back to you months ago. I have no idea where your black cashmere overcoat is, and as I explained to you the last time you demanded to be told of its whereabouts, I can't be held responsible for it, since you bought it after our divorce."

"I shouldn't have married you."

Rebecca didn't flinch. Instead, she spun to face him. "Look, we both wish that, Ray."

"No, no, I'm saying this wrong." His forehead wrinkled. "When I heard you'd remarried, it got me thinking, and when I saw you in line just now, when you turned and looked at me, I remembered why I *did* marry you. We met in a hospital cafeteria line, remember? You had this...radiance, and I wanted that in my life. My parents had just cut me off because I chose dermatology over the family tradition of cardiac surgery. I felt angry and alone and then...there you were."

He'd been handsome and self-deprecating. She'd been lonely and flattered. "But your parents eventually softened and brought you back into the family fold, didn't they? Then you didn't need me anymore. Not only that, but you wanted someone else."

"I never meant to hurt you."

"But you did." What was the point of pretending otherwise? Rebecca thought. "You should have been honest with me if you weren't happy."

"I thought you could feel it, too. I assumed—"

"Never assume, Ray." Bitterness, regret, an ugly sense of failure seeped out of her heart and into her voice. "That's what I learned from you."

"Well." He shrugged his shoulders as if to shrug away the truth and then gave her a bright, fake smile. "You're remarried now. All's well that ends well."

Did it, Ray? she wanted to shout. *Did it end well? Or are you just assuming again?*

Because despite spending the night in Trent's bed, despite the fact that he'd made playful, wonderful, brighter-than-the-stars love to her the night before, she couldn't bring herself to believe there would be any substantive change in their relationship. She didn't *want* herself to start believing in that.

He was still Trent Crosby, rich, powerful CEO. She was still Rebecca, navy brat turned nurse.

It was safer to assume nothing, to depend on nothing and no one except herself.

It was with that sobering thought that she began work and it seemed to color her entire twelve-hour shift. The OR was packed all day long and she never had a chance to sit down or snatch a bite to eat. When her replacement showed up, her only thought was finding someplace where she could hide from herself, her thoughts and Trent.

She was unclipping her name badge and waiting for an elevator when she heard Sydney Aston's voice. "Rebecca, what are you up to?"

"I'm thinking about heading for the airport and buying a one-way ticket to Tahiti." Or at the very least some downtime in her old duplex that was sitting, unoccupied, until she could decide what to do with it. Scrounging up what she hoped was her final smile of the day, Rebecca turned toward her friend.

Sydney was dressed in a sapphire-colored, chic business suit and she carried a huge basket covered in clear wrapping and tied with a cabbage-size bow of pale green ribbon. "No Tahiti until after the baby shower for you. You didn't forget it, did you?"

"Baby shower?" Rebecca frowned, then used the heel of her hand to tap her forehead. Morgan and Emma's baby shower that the PAN group was throwing tonight. "Yes, I did forget."

"Then it's lucky for you that we went in on a gift and that *I* was in charge of buying it." She held up the basket for inspection. "Everything new parents might need."

Rebecca gave an obligatory peek, but then stepped back. "I don't think I'm in a party mood. Maybe I should—"

"Nonsense," Sydney said. "The only way to get in the party mood is to get to the party. Besides, you don't think you can avoid giving us the obligatory details about your quickie marriage forever, do you? Everyone in PAN has been dying to know them. You might as well get it over with."

"That's not an incentive, Sydney."

The other woman held the basket in one arm and latched on to Rebecca's forearm with the other. "Don't worry, I've already passed along that very skimpy account you gave me over the phone. There shouldn't be more than a hundred or so questions still left for people to ask."

Despite herself, Rebecca laughed and let Sydney haul her toward the PAN meeting. But when they were within a few feet of the door, Rebecca could see that the room was packed. Second thoughts flooded her. "Sydney, really. I don't think I can face a crowd tonight."

"Nonsense," her friend said again. With a mischievous smile, she grabbed Rebecca's hand. "There's a surprise inside that I think you'll like."

Warning bells went off. "Surprise?" Pulling her hand from Sydney's, Rebecca jostled the shoulder bag slung over her friend's arm. It tumbled to the ground, spilling some of its contents.

"Oh, Sydney, I'm so sorry." Rebecca crouched down to retrieve the errant items. She stuffed a lipstick, a package of tissues and a pen back inside. Stretching her arm, she snagged a small, leatherbound notepad. As she carried it toward the purse, a piece of paper fluttered free and landed faceup another few feet away. "Whoops."

"I'll get it." Sydney charged forward.

Rebecca was closer, though, and swooped down on it. The paper was a clipping from a magazine, with an eye-catching headline that screamed out, Do You Know Where Your Child Is?

She glanced over at Sydney, who was now staring at the article in Rebecca's hand as if it was a hissing snake. Alarmed, Rebecca began to skim the words, but then Sydney snatched it away and stuffed it in her purse.

"Is there something wrong, Sydney?" The few words she'd been able to read made it clear the story was about unsolved kidnappings. Remembering Nicholas's bad dreams her friend had described at the last PAN get-together, Rebecca felt an icy chill roll down her back. "Is this more than a mother's natural fears? Are you truly worrying that someone's going to try and steal Nicholas?"

"Steal my son?" Sydney shook her head and let loose

a wobbly giggle. "Of course not. Now come on, they're waiting for us in there."

Frowning, Rebecca followed the other woman down the hallway. "Something's wrong."

Sydney shook her head just as they reached the meeting-room doorway. "Two children could have the exact same birthmark, couldn't they?"

"The same birthmark? What?" She turned her head to stare at her friend as they crossed the threshold into the room.

"Surprise!"

Rebecca's head jerked toward the crowd. "What?"

Wearing huge grins, the PAN members were watching her reaction. Her head and body stock-still, Rebecca rolled her eyes toward Sydney. "Why did they just yell 'surprise'?"

"Because it's a surprise." Sydney was smiling now and looked much more like herself. "Can't you see the writing on the wall?"

Rebecca cautiously looked left where a pastel-colored banner read, "We can't wait to meet you, Baby Davis!" The adopted infant Morgan Davis and his wife were expecting any day.

Sydney laughed. "The other wall."

There was the answer. On the opposite side of the room, another banner read: "Best wishes Rebecca and Trent!" And under the dot of the exclamation point was the one person Rebecca had been hoping to avoid to-night.

Her husband.

Her face flushed with heat and went even hotter as he came toward her, winding his way around the tables and the people. As he came to a stop in front of her, cameras flashed.

"Did you know about this?" she whispered.

"I got a call at work today," he answered. His expression was unreadable; his eyes stared straight into hers.

"I don't know what to say." How to act. What to think. Only what not to think.

Assume nothing.

Don't imagine anything has changed.

Don't expect him to be any more your husband than he was before.

Don't believe.

"You forgot something this morning when you left so early," he said.

"I did?" Her face burned again as she remembered having to gather up her clothes from the floor of his room and from the stairway. Had she missed something crucial? "Wh-what did I forget?"

He cupped his hands around her face. "This."

And to the sound of whoops and hollers and whistles from her friends around her, Trent laid on her one fancy, thorough and very, very sweet fairy-tale kiss.

Nine

It was excruciating. The man whom Rebecca had hoped to avoid until she could figure out a way to behave around him was shoulder-to-shoulder with her, guest of honor at a surprise party in celebration of their marriage. A marriage that they'd taken to a new, intimate level the night before.

Staring down at the mound of gifts piled on the table in front of her and Trent, she didn't know where to look or whom to blame.

"Sweetheart?" a voice prodded from a long way off. *"Sweetheart?"*

Rebecca jumped. "Huh?" Her gaze found its way to the tip of Trent's left ear. "What?"

"Did you want to tell them all about our romance, or should I?"

"Huh? What romance?"

"*Our* romance." Chuckling, Trent slanted a smile at the crowd around them and wiggled his eyebrows. "Nothing dreamier than a woman in love, right?"

Rebecca's face burned. *But I'm not in love with you!* Though she could hardly scream it out loud, could she? Oh, but she wanted to. She wanted to assure him that she knew last night had changed nothing essential about their relationship or their views on love. "I'm sorry. I didn't get much sleep last night—"

Rebecca broke off as the group exchanged knowing looks and laughed. She shifted her mortified gaze to Trent's face, and then another wave of embarrassment scorched her. "I mean, I—I—"

His hand came up to give her shoulder a reassuring squeeze. "She means she had a long day at work and wants to know what's inside all these packages." The Davises had already opened all the baby gifts and she and Trent were now in the group's sole spotlight. He slid a beribboned box her way. "Go ahead, honey."

Honey. Sweetheart. Oh, he was good, she thought. He didn't look the least bit discomfited by the situation or by the teasing, despite what had happened between them the night before. As a matter of fact, he looked cool and calm, as if nothing had happened at all.

Because it meant nothing to him, silly.

Yes, that must be it. She focused on unwrapping the package even as the knowledge sank to the pit of her stomach like a heavy weight. Last night hadn't affected him at all.

The proof was in the way he was handling the ongoing PAN inquisition. As she opened the presents—among them were monogrammed towels, a romantic picnic basket for two and crystal candlesticks—he deftly fielded the questions they threw at him. They clamored for the details of how they'd met, how they'd courted, how he'd proposed. She knew she should be jumping in with explanations—these were *her* friends, after all—but Trent didn't appear to need her.

He charmed, he hedged, he negotiated, then he doled out the tiniest of details as if they were concessions on a multibazillion-dollar contract.

She could only marvel at his cool. While her nerve endings were hopping around like teenagers at a high-school dance, not by word or deed did he give away the fact that they'd married for reasons as untraditional and unromantic as a shared cynicism about love.

Rebecca sneaked another peek at him as he fibbed about how he'd taken one look at her "valentine face" and fallen hard. Valentine—wasn't that laying it on a bit thick? But everyone seemed to be buying his baloney.

The thought made her tension ease a little. On the one hand, it seemed a bit insulting that sharing a bed with him left him so unaffected that he could blather on. But on the other hand, his composed demeanor was reassuring. If last night had meant so little to him, then she didn't have to worry that he'd expect a repeat.

Because that seemed like much too big a risk to take—for their agreement, for her heart.

She reached for the last package.

"Oh, Rebecca," someone called out from the back of the crowd. "Let Trent open that one."

Something about the laugh in that someone's voice gave her pause. She made a big show of looking at her watch. "Look how late it is! We'll just take this home as is and—"

"Nuh-uh-uh," her co-worker and PAN member, Peggy, said, pushing to the front of the group. There was a mischievous grin on her face. "That one's from me and I want Trent to do the honors."

Rebecca swallowed. "Oh. Okay. Sure." What was Peggy up to? Rebecca didn't know, but with wickedness glinting in her friend's eye, she was more than thrilled to pass the gift over to Mr. Fluster-Free.

Whatever it was, he'd handle it with aplomb.

Trent took the gift from Rebecca like the cool customer he'd demonstrated himself to be. Wearing a half smile, he made short work of the silver paper. Beneath the box's lid was a wealth of star-spangled tissue. And beneath *that*...

Trent froze.

Goose bumps burst across Rebecca's skin. "What is it?" she heard herself ask anxiously. "What?" She didn't know if she was more worried about the contents of the package or the change in Trent. His calm was *her* guarantee that things between them hadn't changed.

Both his hands reached into the package and came

out with red satin spaghetti straps hooked around his forefingers. A red satin scandalous nothing of a shortie negligee dangled from them.

Rebecca's stomach jittered as she watched Trent's face.

Then he grinned. A natural, easy, I'm-a-guy grin. "Look, honey," he said to Rebecca, turning to give her a full view of the embarrassing garment. "It says His."

And sure enough it did. Rebecca felt hot color crawling up her neck as she took in the three letters, *H-I-S,* embroidered in black like a Miss America banner across the skimpy lingerie's front. Without her permission, a fancy flared to life in her imagination. Herself in that red satin nothing. Trent's hand tracing those emphatic letters.

H-I-S. His. *His.*

She remembered the night before. Trent's hands on her. Trent's mouth on her skin. Beneath her practical scrubs, her nipples peaked and the place between her thighs went warm and heavy. Oh. Oh, no. This wasn't good. This wasn't the smart way to handle things.

But she wanted him again. She wanted him bad, no matter that it seemed better not to take a chance on getting so close to him another time.

Her gaze lifted to Trent's face. His expression betrayed nothing but good-natured humor. How could he be so undisturbed? How could what they'd shared together not even spark a flicker of sexual heat? Suddenly, the calm depths of his eyes irritated her.

If he could pretend for the PAN members they were a real couple, the least he could do was pretend for *her* that last night lingered somewhere in his mind. Okay, it wasn't her most logical thought, but this was another of those life moments where logic was unnecessary, if not downright unwelcome.

"There's more!" Peggy said.

Rebecca looked over at her friend. "More?"

Oh, she hoped that meant what she thought. She stepped nearer Trent and leaned toward the box, making sure her breast skimmed his forearm. Her upward glance showed not one single twitch of the muscles in his face. Gritting her teeth, she returned her focus to what was nestled in the spangled tissue. She snatched it up, then straightened, brushing against him once more.

"Look, darling," she said, pasting on her own non-committal smile. With two fingers, she pulled the skinny, elastic sides apart so that the G-string hung between her hands. "This one says Hers."

But once again his expression showed nothing more than a mild interest. Didn't the man have a memory? Had he got up and gone to work all day without giving a thought to what they'd done together? Didn't red satin bring up a fantasy or two?

Feeling even more miffed, she pretended to inspect the minuscule satin pouch suspended in the air between her hands. "Though it looks to be a little too big."

The men in the room gave a collective wince.

Trent's "valentine" gave him her most innocent, sugary smile.

Trent laughed with more of that calm good nature. "Take this as a warning, my friends. Don't leave your socks balled up on the bedroom floor. Your wife will find a way to get you back every time."

Rebecca wanted to stamp her foot at his complete self-possession. She wanted to get a rise out of him. She wanted to see him sweat, to see him show *some* reaction over what had happened between them the night before. Why was she the only one who remembered it was incredible, indelible, scary?

"There's one last thing in the box," Peggy put in again. "You won't want to miss it."

Without hesitation, Trent put his hand into the tissue and pulled out a book. He held it up and read the title aloud. *"Sexploration: A His and Hers..."* His voice lowered, hoarsened, and his gaze jumped from what was in his hand to Rebecca's face. *"...Atlas."*

Expressions chased across his face.

His eyes narrowed and seemed to burn with the heat of a sexual flame. She read the thoughts racing through his mind.

What's the capital of Rhode Island?
Rebecca, here's Mt. Hood.
You feel so good.
This making-babies business is beautiful.

A flush spread across his cheekbones and his nostrils flared. Rebecca took a step back, crushing the G-string in one fist. Ignoring her retreat, he grabbed her wrist, then looked at the people around them.

"Rebecca's right. It's late. We have to go now." He started pulling her around the table, his fingers like a gentle but immovable vise on her arm.

"Oh, Trent," Peggy singsonged.

He was parting the crowd with the sheer force of his intent. "What?" He didn't pause to look at the other woman.

"Aren't you forgetting your gifts?"

That halted him. "Yes," he said. "Thanks." And he swung back, snatched up the red negligee, then towed Rebecca out of the room.

She heard the burst of amused chatter as they exited. Glancing over her shoulder, she saw grins on several faces. Peggy caught her eye, smiled, then sent her a wiggly-fingered wave.

It was the last friendly face Rebecca saw. Trent pulled her out of the hospital so fast that everyone else she encountered was a mere blur. The next thing she knew, she was seat-belted beside him in his car and he was speeding out of the hospital parking lot. Her behind bounced on the leather seat as he took a speed bump without a touch of foot to brake.

She opened her mouth to protest, but then looked at him and thought better of it. Though they'd just left her car in the parking lot, she'd mention the need to retrieve it another time. He was driving with both hands on the wheel, that scrap of satin fabric pooled in his lap. Her fingers loosened on the matching scrap in her hand.

"What the *hell* did you think you were doing?"

Her gaze jerked toward him. He was staring out the windshield, his expression hard. "I, um, I…" She glanced down at the G-string for inspiration. Such a little thing to have caused her such trouble. At least she assumed that's what he was angry about. "I was just kidding—"

"You were *teasing* me, baby, using sex to tease me, and that can be dangerous when my temper's already frayed."

His temper was *frayed?* He was *dangerous?* To her, he'd appeared to be in glacial control. "Well, I, um, I had no idea you'd had a bad day at work, Trent."

"A bad day at work? You think I had a bad day at work?"

He repeated it with such quiet precision that she didn't know what to think. "You didn't?"

"Baby, my bad day started when I woke up to find you'd run out on me." He cast her a fuming sidelong look. "I'm accustomed to a little more consideration from my bed partners."

"Well, I—"

"I happen to think that a good night like we shared deserves a 'Good morning.'"

"I see—"

"Do you?" He pulled into their driveway and shut off the engine. Then he turned to stare straight into her eyes. "Then maybe you can see your way to telling me why you took off like that."

Again, Rebecca's nerve endings started dancing around to the rhythm of a hip-hop song only they could hear.

His eyes narrowed. "Well?"

Okay, so he wasn't unaffected by their night together, after all. As a matter of fact, now he looked angry and frustrated and so attractive that she worried he might soon guess the way her skin was heating and her heart was beating.

His nostrils flared again. Oh, yeah, he suspected, all right. And she had the sudden, certain thought that he wasn't going to think returning to separate bedrooms was the good idea that she did.

Trent lifted an eyebrow.

Rebecca crowded the passenger door.

If he wasn't so damn mad at her, maybe he'd feel guilty for that apprehensive look on her face. But, hell, they'd made a baby last night and this morning she'd skipped out, treating what they'd had, treating *him*, like a one-night stand.

"I left messages for you," he ground out.

Her eyes widened. "You did? I was so busy today I didn't even think to check."

He made himself take a deep breath. "What *were* you thinking, Rebecca?"

She grimaced. "I was hoping you wouldn't want to take the mature, let's-discuss-this-new-wrinkle route."

His head dropped back against the rest. "You don't have much of an opinion of me, do you?"

"No!" She reached out and touched his arm. "It's me. I didn't—don't know what to say about last night. What to think."

He looked over at her. Her gaze instantly fell, landing on the ridiculous G-string. "At least you can assure me you don't really think that stupid thing is too big for me."

A smile played at the corners of her lips. Trent remembered the taste of her mouth, sweet and warm. He remembered her soft curls nestled against his heart.

"I shouldn't have said that," she replied, peeking up at him from beneath her lashes. "I'm not very good at this, Trent."

"'This'?"

She shrugged one shoulder, setting a line of little ducks printed on her scrubs to waddling. "You said you expect more consideration from your bed partners. I haven't had much experience with bed partners. Nobody since my divorce."

He blinked. "I thought you've been divorced for a while."

"Three years next month."

Saliva pooled in his mouth. His convulsive swallow sent it down the wrong pipe, initiating a fit of coughing. Nurse Rebecca, of course, knew just where to whack his back, but it still took a few minutes to get his wheezing to calm down.

"You need a glass of water," she said when he could breathe normally again. Her fingers went for the door handle.

His fingers went for her thigh. "Rebecca, we can't go back to the way things were before."

He heard the little hitch in her breathing. "Trent, I don't know—"

"I do. I know that I can't live in that house and not have you in my arms and in my bed. It makes what we have better, don't you think?"

She stared down at his hand on her leg, as if the sight fascinated her.

It fascinated the hell out of him, because just a few inches away was the heaven he wanted to spend the rest of the night exploring. Without that damn atlas.

"What we have…?"

"A partnership. A marriage. A baby," he answered. "We worked pretty well as a team tonight, wouldn't you say?"

She nodded. "You did well with my friends."

"I like your friends. Several of them I already know, by the way. And you did well with my family yester-day."

"Your sister Katie and her husband, you mean. I haven't met any of the others."

He waved away her concerns. "They'll all feel the same way. The point, Rebecca, is that we deal well to-gether. Out in the world. In bed."

Beneath his hand, the muscles of her thigh twitched. "I wish you'd stop saying that," she whispered.

"Bed?" He laughed. "Since I woke up this morning I haven't been able to get my mind out of it, how we were together in it." And how, when he realized she'd run out on him, taking every sign that she'd been there with her, he'd begun to suspect she'd turned coward on him.

It wasn't going to last, though. Now their lives to-gether included sex, and he for one was damn glad about it. Neither one of them would be content to go backward, no matter what she thought. They'd both be better off; he'd prove it to her. Not to mention he was certain the people who worked for him would be happy to have a boss relieved of all the tension that had been building inside of him.

"Let's go inside," Trent said, changing tactics. *Give her some time to get used to the idea.* Pushing her wasn't necessary. Besides, if he couldn't persuade her to his way of thinking, then he didn't deserve her in his bed. And she didn't belong there.

But she did belong there, he thought as he walked with her through the front door and then led the way toward the kitchen. His eye caught on the vase of yellow tulips on the dining-room table. Rebecca had removed the clear glass beads that usually anchored the waxy flowers in a soldierlike posture. They lazed in the glass vase now, almost lolling, looking, for the first time, natural and fresh.

Like Rebecca. The thought made his gut tighten. Struck by a sudden, new appreciation of her, he spun toward her and grabbed her shoulders. Her little "oh" of surprise gave him the perfect opening for his tongue. He thrust it inside her mouth, and the kiss that had been in his mind as something almost affectionate transformed into a hot intimacy that had him hard and aching in seconds. Lifting his head, he stared down at her red, swollen lips.

She blinked at him, her hands clutching his forearms. "What was that for?"

"Proof."

"Proof?"

That we're about sex, sweetheart. He didn't know

why the notion of it made his shoulders relax and that strange knot in his stomach unclench. "Hungry?" he asked, letting her go with a smile. They needed fuel for how he planned they'd spend the night ahead.

She swayed, and he grabbed her forearms again to steady her.

"Are you okay?" he asked.

"I'm fine." She tucked a lock of hair behind her ear. "Did you mention food?"

"Soup and grilled cheese?" He smoothed her hair over her forehead, distracted by the way one of her soft waves clung to his fingers. "I think it's my cooking night."

"That sounds good." Her gaze on his face, she backed away from him. "I'll just change out of my uniform."

He let her get as far as the bottom of the stairs before he stopped her. "Rebecca."

She looked over. "Yes?"

"Why don't you put this on?" He tossed something at her.

On reflex she caught it. Her face flamed as she realized it was the red satin nightie. "I…you…" With further speech apparently beyond her, she shot him a look and headed up the staircase.

He laughed and turned toward the kitchen, satisfied he'd signaled his intent. Whether she came down in the negligee or not, he'd see her in his bed tonight.

"Trent? *Trent?*" It sounded as if she was calling from the top of the stairs.

He stuck his head out the kitchen door. "Yeah?"

"My clothes aren't where they should be."

Oh, right. He'd nearly forgotten that maneuver he'd dreamed up this morning when he'd been pissed at her for leaving him without a word. Keeping his voice calm and pleasant, he called back to her. "Sure, they are. They're in your room."

Your new room.

She was silent a moment. Then, "Trent Crosby, what did you do?"

He grinned. Okay, he was a high-handed, arrogant bastard. But he'd always considered those his good points. He heard Rebecca move away from the staircase. Still grinning, he listened to her footsteps above him, following her progress along the upstairs hallway to the master bedroom. His bedroom.

Their bedroom, now that he'd moved all her clothes from her closet into his.

How long would it take before she came down to read him the riot act? Or would she be glad that he'd removed the decision from her hands?

"You know I'm right, baby," he murmured, one ear still cocked for what she'd do next. "We're married, we sizzle, so what could be more natural?"

By the end of the night she'd realize she belonged in his bed.

From overhead came a loud thump. The sound of something heavy falling to the floor. Bigger than a shoe. Larger than a lamp. Not an angry noise.

But an unnatural sound.

"Rebecca?" He was calling her name, and already running, though he couldn't say exactly why his instincts were sounding a loud alarm.

"Rebecca?" he shouted, taking the steps by threes. *"Rebecca!"*

But she couldn't reply, not when she was lying slumped in the middle of the bedroom floor.

"We need a doctor. A specialist. A health-care professional," Trent said, his hands gathering up Rebecca's where they lay loosely clasped on the coverlet of his bed. "We need to take you to one."

"Trent, I *am* a health-care professional, remember? It's nothing. I fainted because I didn't eat today."

He glared at her, then reached over for the pack of crackers she'd asked for once he'd lifted her onto the bed and she'd opened her eyes. "And why the hell is that?"

She shrugged. "It was that kind of day."

"There will be no more days like that, do you understand? You gave me two dozen more gray hairs."

Rebecca's hand stroked through his hair and she gave him a little smile. "You're silly. Where's this alleged gray?"

He grabbed her fingers and held her palm against his cheek. "You need to rest."

"I need to eat."

That got him to his feet. "Steak, baked potatoes, and lima beans are on their way. I'm going to call De-Luce's."

"Lima beans?" She made a face. "You don't eat anything green, yet you want me to ingest lima beans? I thought you mentioned soup. That sounds perfect."

"Sounds," he muttered. "Don't mention sounds to me." The sound of her dropping to the floor above him would follow him for the rest of his life, he knew. Leaning down, he tucked the covers more closely about her legs. "I'm going to get your dinner. Are you warm enough?"

"I'm fine, Mom."

He frowned at her, her smile doing nothing to lighten his mood. "You're the mom, damn it. You should be taking better care of yourself."

"I will," she promised. "But tonight you're doing a pretty great job. Thanks."

"Stay put," he said, frowning at her again. "I'll be in the kitchen. Call if you need me."

He ran down the stairs and into the kitchen, then opened the soup and put it to simmering on the stove. Call. The person who needed to call was him. His fingers clumsy, he punched Katie's number and listened in frustration and worry to the ringing phone. *What should I do for her?* he practiced saying in his head.

What should I do for me? That was what he wanted to ask, too. He was supposed to be having sex with his wife, not brooding over her. Not worrying about her. Not caring so much about her.

Katie's answering machine clicked on and he slammed down the phone. He couldn't call his other pregnancy expert, his littlest sister, Ivy, because the time difference meant she'd be asleep now. So would her baby, he thought, and Ivy would give him a verbal lashing if he woke the child. Stirring the soup, he tried talking himself into a better frame of mind.

Rebecca fainted. She's fine. She's mine.

The last thought scared the hell out of him, so he took his mind out of his heart and tried putting it into the gutter. *She's mine, all right. Think of the red satin nightie.* Not tonight, but soon, soon he'd see her wearing it.

But even that didn't conjure up any comforting images. Instead he could only picture her curled up on his floor in that goofy duck-wear. His valentine crumpled on the floor.

His.

She's mine.

He grabbed the phone, desperate for help. Punching out the familiar number, he didn't even try to plan ahead of time what he would say. When the familiar voice answered, he blurted out the first thing that came into his head. "My wife fainted and I don't know what to do."

There was a long silence. "This isn't the tyrannical troll that lives in the next office, is it?"

"Claudine, it's me. Trent. I—"

I'm not comfortable with this. I don't want to feel this way.

"Claudine, I need help. Please."

Ten

After a steaming bowl of minestrone soup, Trent brought Rebecca a woman. More specifically, a woman who looked familiar.

"This is my secretary," he said, ushering her into the bedroom. "Claudine."

Short and squarely built, Claudine had a head of thick silver hair that contrasted with her black eyebrows and dark eyes. The eyes crinkled at the corners when she smiled at Rebecca, shoving Trent out of the way at the same time. "I'm your *assistant*. We're supposed to remember that, aren't we?"

He shook his head, watching Claudine bustle forward. "We will remember that when you stop calling me, we."

Without looking at him, she waved him off. "Go away. Find something useful to do."

He scowled, retreating to the doorway. "Nag."

"Donkey."

"Witch."

"Donkey's hindquarters."

Despite the insults traded, Rebecca could see, with a strange glee, Trent still hovered. "Claudine, are you sure...?"

His assistant's voice and expression softened. "Go. Take a drive or something. We'll be fine here."

She didn't have to ask him again. Trent disappeared.

Once alone with the other woman, Rebecca wasn't sure what to say, however. "I'm sorry that he called and asked you to come. I told him I was fine."

Claudine perched on the edge of the bed. "He panicked, that's all."

"Trent, panic?" It didn't seem conceivable that the big, bad businessman could ever lose his cool. "He doesn't look panicked to me."

"Learned that iron control from his father. But he can't fool me. I've worked with him for almost a decade and I worked with Jack Crosby before that."

Rebecca shook her head. "If you say so. But I still don't know why he had to drag you over here."

Claudine smiled once more, those dark eyes of hers twinkling. "I didn't mind getting a chance to see you again, this time as Trent's bride."

"Oh, well, about that..." Each time she had to present herself as his wife, it was getting harder, not easier to pull off. "We, uh, we…"

Get it together, Rebecca.

"We have a lot in common." *Lie. They had one thing in common, and that was their avowed pessimism about love.*

Claudine nodded as if what Rebecca had said aloud made some kind of sense. "He tells me you're pregnant."

"Oh!" Another wave of awkwardness flooded over her. She'd just tried to pull off the happily married-couple thing when all along Trent's assistant knew the truth. "Well, I…we…"

Claudine leaned over to pat her hand. "I came of age in the sixties, Rebecca. I've heard of premarital sex."

Maybe Trent's assistant *didn't* know the truth. "I'm just a couple of months along."

"And that can be the hardest time of all in a pregnancy," Claudine asserted. "You're tired. You're hungry. You're not hungry. You're still tired. And though you don't *look* any different, you're starting to feel very, very different."

Rebecca relaxed against the pillows. "I take it you're a mother?"

"Four boys. Men now. But you don't forget how it is to be pregnant, especially that first time. It can be frightening, like finding yourself on a train that not only never slows down, but has no stops, either."

"Yes," Rebecca said, smiling. "I feel that way, not just about the pregnancy, but about…" Her voice trailed away as she realized what she was about to say.

"About the marriage?" Claudine prompted. "That's

natural, too. I'd known my husband all my life, but I remember looking at him across the table on the second day of our honeymoon and thinking he was a stranger. A complete, total stranger. I wanted to run home to my mother."

Rebecca laughed. "And did you?"

Claudine shook her head. "My head might have seen a stranger but my heart still knew who he was."

My heart knew who he was. The words echoed inside of Rebecca. She didn't want her heart involved in her marriage. She didn't.

"That's why Trent called me, you know."

Rebecca blinked. "What?"

"He thought you might be missing your mother right about now. He said she'd passed away, but he hoped that another woman, an older one, might be able to give you some comfort."

The corners of Rebecca's eyes stung. "He did? He said that?" Her nose was tingling and she had to rub it. "That's so sweet."

"I thought so myself," Claudine said. "I also thought it was testament to his feelings for you. This is a man who lives and breathes his business, but he's been coming up for air, real air, since he married you."

Yes, but Trent doesn't have any feelings for me, Rebecca thought. At least not the warm, fuzzy kind. But she couldn't say that, of course. Her eyes stung again. "He's going to be a good father."

Claudine nodded. "He is. He takes his responsibilities very seriously. Even some responsibilities that aren't his."

"Robbie Logan," Rebecca murmured. "And his brother Danny's little boy."

The other woman nodded again. "There are so many who see Trent as heartless, while I think it's that big heart of his that he's always desperate to keep well-protected."

Even though she doubted the assertion, Rebecca was mortified to feel a tear roll down her cheek. "Hormones," she said, laughing as she wiped it away.

Then Trent was in the doorway again, a brown paper bag in his arms. "Damn it, Claudine. I didn't bring you over here to make my wife cry."

The older woman smiled at Rebecca but didn't let a beat go by. "It's because I just told her the amount of my measly salary, you ungrateful tightwad." She got to her feet. "Now it's time for me to go home and search the want ads for a second job so I can keep up with inflation."

"I heard the Portland Playhouse is holding auditions for *The Wizard of Oz*. You could try out for the Wicked Witch of the West."

She sailed toward him, her chin high. "Cad."

"Shrew."

"Brute."

"Crone."

She smiled as she past him. "Malefactor."

Trent froze. "Okay, fine," he said, his voice sulky. "That point's yours."

Claudine sent Rebecca a triumphant look over her shoulder. "They always are. Good night, Rebecca!"

With her pulse racing and her stomach feeling as if she was on a long elevator fall, it was all Rebecca could do to give a little wave. Then, clasping her hands tightly together, she paid careful attention to Trent, who sat himself down on the other side of the bed.

Don't give yourself away, she thought as she watched him rummaging in his bag. His short hair was a bit mussed, as if he'd scraped his hands through its earlier perfect order.

He tossed a couple of magazines on her lap. "I didn't know if you were a *Cosmo* or a *Vogue* girl, so I got them both."

Her throat was too dry to thank him. He didn't know if she was a *Cosmo* or a *Vogue* girl. But it didn't seem to matter, because she was dizzy with this terrible thing that was happening to her.

Out of Trent's bag came two pints of Ben & Jerry's ice cream. "Phish Phood for you, Chubby Hubby for me."

She managed to find her voice. Maybe she could will this moment into normalcy, maybe she could will away this horrible, calamitous, dangerous disaster that was happening to her. "What if *I* want the Chubby Hubby?"

He grinned at her. "Then you'll have him, if I eat many pints of this stuff."

It wasn't going away. She couldn't will it away.

He set the ice cream aside and then he swung his long legs onto the bed. Reaching behind him, he adjusted the pillows so that he was propped up beside her. Rebecca breathed in, smelling Trent's lime-soap scent, the June evening air, a whiff of mingled perfumes from the inserts in the magazines on her lap. They filled her head like the notes of a song and she knew it was music she'd never forget.

The bag rattled as Trent slid his hand inside again. "I thought we could have some fun with this tonight." He held up a book. *Baby Names: The Good, the Bad and the Out-and-Out Ugly.*

And if she hadn't already fallen, that would have shoved her over. Why? Because the attractive, intense man who'd driven her home earlier tonight had had sex on his mind. But now, the tender protector who was stretched out beside her was willing to spend the evening with her playing Name that Baby.

But the fact was she already *had* fallen. Sometime between the minestrone and the music sounding in her head. Maybe when she'd found out he'd wanted to give her a mother in the guise of his assistant. But, no. "It was the malefactor that did it," she murmured.

He frowned. "What?"

That look on his face when Claudine had bested him. Crestfallen, little-boy sulky, yet still man enough to acknowledge some other winner. Maybe it was silly. Maybe it was a secret she'd always keep. Maybe she'd never be able to tell her grandchildren the moment she'd fallen in love with their grandfather.

But that was it.

"I want to know when I'm going to meet this wife of yours," Trent's mother said. "Why didn't you bring her to dinner tonight?"

"Because she had a long day at work and I thought she'd rather stay home and rest." Not that he'd asked Rebecca. He'd told her he had a business dinner and that he'd be home late. All his dinners with his mother ran late, because it took hours to get her complaints out of her system.

"Maybe I should call her and have her meet me for lunch at the country club."

Trent didn't look up from his prime rib. If he showed alarm, then his mother would make sure she did that very thing. "I'd rather you wouldn't, Mom," he said in a mild tone.

"Are you ashamed of me?" Sheila demanded.

"Of course not." He lifted his gaze, taking in the beauty that a plastic surgeon was paid a fortune to preserve. Injections vanquished the lines of discontent on her face. Creams softened her skin and bleached away the marks of age. Her neck was as smooth as the blade of a scalpel. Shame wasn't the emotion his mother brought out in him.

"Are you ashamed of Rachel, then?"

"Rebecca," Trent corrected with an inward shake of his head. "Her name is Rebecca, and I'm not ashamed of her, either."

"But a *nurse*, Trent. Couldn't you have found yourself someone more…stylish?"

"Maybe you could do something about that for me, Mom. Talk to the administrators at the hospital and see if they can bring on board Stella McCartney to design the scrubs the staff wear."

"Scrubs." Nose wrinkling, his mother lifted her wineglass and took a sip of the triple-digit bottle of pinot grigio she'd ordered because he'd be paying for it. "That very word makes my point."

Trent mentally tightened the armor he donned before any encounter with his mother and let the asinine comment run off his back. Katie had questioned him about why he put himself through these meetings with their mother, but she didn't understand.

First, she *was* their mother. As the oldest, the oldest son, he couldn't shake off the sense of duty that he felt toward her.

Second, she'd found out about his marriage. Flown from her home in Palm Springs, or so she said, just to offer her congratulations. If he hadn't agreed to have dinner with her, her curiosity would have led her to contact Rebecca for sure. This way, he hoped to put his mother off that idea. Sheila wasn't really interested in Trent's wife, only in how his marriage would affect her.

If he continued his duty dinners when necessary, then he hoped she'd otherwise stay out of his life.

His mother took another sip from her glass. "I always liked your first wife, Mara. What happened?"

"Mara left me, Mom, remember?"

"That's right." She nodded. "Because you didn't have time for her. Too wrapped up in the business, just like your-father-the-bastard."

And last but not least, Trent had to admit that he'd agreed to this dinner in order to remind himself what his mother was like, what Mara was like, what women could be like. What could happen when you made the mistake of exposing your underbelly to the female half of the world.

He was a pessimist. So sue him.

"By the way, how *is* your-father-the bastard and that bimbo he married?"

"Dad's well, Mom, and Toni, too. I'll tell them you asked." Trent forced himself to cut another bite of his meal, put it in his mouth and chew.

"Don't you do any such thing, Trent Crosby. I wouldn't care if that man was going in for a quadruple bypass tomorrow, not after the way he's treated me!"

"Boy, it's sure great to see you, Mom," Trent said, picking up his glass and toasting her. "It's as if no time has passed at all."

She narrowed her eyes. Sheila was selfish but not stupid. "Don't take that tone of voice with me, Trent. Danny is bad enough."

Trent froze, then carefully set down his knife and fork. "You've been talking to Danny?" His little brother didn't need any more grief in his life. "I wish you wouldn't, Mom."

She speared a bite of her squab. "You wish I wouldn't meet your new wife, and you wish I wouldn't talk to your brother. My very own son! You don't always get what you wish for, Trent."

"Don't I know it," he muttered. He lifted his water glass and tried to swallow back the headache that was beginning to drum at the back of his neck. If he could get what he wished for, his mother would be tucked away in Palm Springs and he would be tucked away in his house with Rebecca—in bed. But since she'd fainted the week before, he'd kept his distance. He stayed at work late, coming home long after she was asleep—in his room. He told her he'd been sleeping in the guest bed so that he wouldn't disturb her.

He'd been sleeping in the guest bed because *she* disturbed *him*.

"Trent?"

His gaze jerked up. "Excuse me, Mom. What did you say?"

"I asked you about the Summer Solstice dance at the country club Saturday night. Are you going?"

Still distracted by thoughts of Rebecca, Trent's mind drifted away. "Hmm? Yeah. Sure. I bought a table." The night before, he'd been tempted to wake his wife when he'd finally wandered home in the dead of night. Seventeen straight hours at his desk hadn't dampened his desire for her.

He remembered every detail of her body from their one night together—the sleek warmth of her skin, the weighty surprise of her breasts, the clinging sweetness of her wavy hair. He'd wanted to anchor his hands in it, twine his fingers with it and hold her against the pillow to take his kiss, wakening Sleeping Beauty to all that he wanted to softly, gently, tenderly give her.

But that was the danger. All that softness, gentleness, tenderness. Giving her that would mean first dropping the protection—the breastplate, the chain mail—that had kept him invulnerable since Robbie had gone missing. Since Danny's Noah had been kidnapped. Since Mara had left him with nothing more than a vial of empty dreams.

Until Rebecca.

But he'd promised himself, promised *her*, that their marriage would be based on strength. On the strength of the notion that love was too nebulous to build a marriage upon. He couldn't go back to her now and say he'd been wrong. That he'd made a mistake.

For God's sake, he *wasn't* mistaken about love.

Katie and Ivy seemed happy enough, but that was the girls. Maybe they were smarter than he was. Hell, braver.

Believing in the unbelievable.

Taking chances on faith.

Risking hurt, risking hearts, when all signs pointed to the fact that love didn't last. That it died. That it didn't, in fact, exist at all.

The rest of the meal with his mother went well enough. He parried when he had to. Threw up a shield when it was necessary. Stood between Sheila and his sisters as he'd done all his life. Not that Ivy's King Max or Katie's Peter would let their mother-in-law do her damage any longer, Plus, he supposed the girls could do fine on their own.

It was just that old habits died hard. Old fears, too.

They were sipping coffee and he was playing with a slice of cheesecake when Sheila brought up the Summer Solstice dance again. "Will your-father-the-bastard be there?"

Trent looked up. "We're sitting together."

"With the bimbo?"

"With Toni, yes."

His mother nodded. "Then I must have a new dress."

Trent set his fork down. "You're going?"

"Of course. I told you that half an hour ago. Weren't you listening?"

Apparently not. Apparently she'd mentioned it when he'd been fantasizing about Rebecca. "I don't want a scene, Mom." That jungle-drums headache was starting up again.

"I don't know what you're talking about."

He couldn't afford to leave it at that. Not when his father and his father's wife were going to be there. Not when Katie and Peter would be in attendance. None of them needed the embarrassment of any tricks Sheila might be capable of producing. Rebecca's second thoughts about their marriage would rise again. She'd tell him it was a mistake and he wouldn't be able to deny it. "Mom, remember when we had that little talk about rumors and Children's Connection? About how I'd revoke your membership at the club if you started any? Well, the same goes if you make a scene at the Summer Solstice dance."

She tried a collagen-enhanced pout on him. "I don't know why you'd say such a thing."

His gaze was steady on hers. "I mean it, Mom. Don't approach Dad."

Her eyes dropped. "Oh, fine. But maybe I wanted to say hello. You know, for old times' sake."

"Right. Old times' sake." Trent didn't bother excising the cynicism from his voice. "The old times were hell, Mom, and you know it."

"It was what happened with that Robbie Logan," she complained. "It put so much stress on your father and me."

Trent sighed. "Whatever, Mom."

"You think you know everything about the past, Trent. But I loved your father once. I loved him very much. And sometimes I wonder if…" A faraway look came into her eyes.

Trent's jaw dropped. In a hundred years, a thousand years, a million years, he wouldn't have believed Sheila would ever have admitted to loving her husband at one time. And from the look on her face…Trent wondered if her bitterness and her complaints masked a hurt that he'd never guessed before.

His mother might not be a nice person. She certainly wasn't an altruistic one. But she was human.

And…she'd loved? She'd loved. And maybe, buried deep beneath her own brand of armor, she still did.

If Trent could believe *that,* then maybe he also had to believe that love existed after all. Could that be possible?

No, damn it, no. Because love could risk all that he was building with Rebecca.

Something woke Rebecca out of a deep sleep. She opened her eyes, listening for the sound of Trent moving into the bedroom that had once been hers. But the noises weren't upstairs noises. They didn't sound like Trent noises either.

On his other late nights he'd always headed straight for the steps. Once at the top, he would stop in the entry of the master bedroom where she'd left the door ajar. She'd know he was there, watching her, and she'd squeeze her eyes shut as her heart squeezed in uncertainty.

And in that same moment, she wanted him, loved him, wanted to dance in delirious circles because love had fallen into her lap.

She wanted him, loved him, wanted to cry in a tantrum of despair because love had fallen into her lap.

After a few minutes of watching her faked sleep, he'd move on, into the other bedroom. And she'd press the one tear she allowed herself against the pillowcase.

But the noises, the non-Trent noises, weren't moving up the stairs tonight. Fear flickered in her throat and she reached for the phone. It was the cordless kind, and she held it against her thumping heart.

The rustling downstairs didn't abate.

Was it a vandal? Burglar? Serial killer in a hockey mask?

Or an idiot woman imagining things? She'd been reading that very spooky romantic suspense book right before turning out her light.

Still gripping the phone, Rebecca slipped out of bed. Then she tiptoed to the top of the stairs and listened. Rustling, all right. From the den, where there was not only the cardboard cottage she'd been making slow progress on, but also where Trent kept his big-screen TV, his stereo, his techie, rich-guy toys that she'd been so intimidated by that she left them solely to the house-keeper to dust.

We'll call 9-1-1, Eisenhower.

And then feel like a complete fool when the police arrested the homeowner for rustling around in his own house.

Gathering her common sense and a little courage, she made her way, noiselessly, down the stairs. From there she scurried across the foyer and through the dining room to peek into the den.

What she saw inside made her take a hasty step back.

Then she peeked in again, confirming her first glimpse.

Her cottage. Her cottage had changed. Half believing she'd find those little mice-turned-dressmakers from Cinderella had turned into construction workers to transform her playhouse, she walked into the den. But instead of mice, the architect was Trent. He stood with his back to her, jacket off, sleeves rolled up, shoeless.

Trent, messing with her house!

She marched forward. "What are you doing?"

He whirled. One of his front shirttails had come loose from his pants. "I, uh, I…"

Propping her hands on her hips, she tilted back her head to take in all he'd done. Her quaint, cute little cottage had a whole new demeanor. It had two stories. A turret. She pointed. "Is that a *drawbridge?*"

He glanced over, and a grin quirked the corners of his mouth. "Yeah. What do you think?"

"What do I *think?*" She stared at him, feeling shabby and rumpled in her old flannel nightshirt while he looked designer-disheveled and downright tickled by his renovations of *her* project.

It was too much. He was too much. He'd taken her humble playhouse and made it into something fantastical.

"How could you?" she said, glaring at him. "How could you do this to—to—" *Me.*

Trent frowned, glanced at the playhouse again. "You don't like it?"

"No, I don't like it. And I don't like—" *What you've done to me. I don't like it that you overturned my modest expectations for our relationship and made me want you to love me like I love you.*

Looking at his gorgeous, puzzled, beloved face, she burst into tears.

Eleven

Trent rushed toward the sobbing Rebecca. "Sweetheart, what's the matter?" He moved to put his arms around her, but she shook her head and backed away from him. Tears were running from her big, Disney-character eyes, and they drenched him with guilt and confusion.

"Is it the playhouse? If you don't like it, I'll put it back the way it was."

She shook her head again.

"Then I'll flatten the whole thing."

"N-no." She covered her face with her hands. "Never mind."

Never mind? Yeah, right. "Rebecca—"

Her hands fell from her face. "Go to bed," she said,

her voice thick. "Or go to work or go out to another business dinner. Just go away and leave me alone!"

Go to work? Go to another business dinner? Maybe what he'd done wrong *was* to leave her alone. "Rebecca, talk to me. What's the matter? If it isn't the playhouse—"

"It *is* the playhouse!" She glowered at him, then wiped her face on her sleeve. "It was simple, it was unassuming, and now it's something else altogether and it's all your fault."

"Then we'll put it back the way it was."

"You can't," she said, her voice resigned. "You can never put it back the way it was."

He nodded in understanding. "This is another one of those times when using logic would be a bad idea, right?"

That startled a laugh out of her. "Oh, I hate when you do that."

"Do what?"

"Make me laugh." She swiped her sleeve over her face. "Especially because I really, really want to be mad at you right now. And don't ask me why."

"Why?"

"Uuuuhh!" Her arms lifted from her sides, fell back. "This isn't the way it's supposed to be. You're not the way you're supposed to be." She crossed to the nearby couch and flopped onto it.

Trent followed her, then sat down himself.

"Why did you do it?" she asked, nodding to the play castle.

"I came home, I couldn't sleep." Not with the left-overs of uneasiness and uncertainty he'd brought home from his dinner with his mother.

Rebecca crossed her arms over her chest. "Things always have to be bigger and better for you, don't they?"

Frowning, he focused back on her. "It wasn't like that. I had an idea—"

"Don't you see how wrong we are together? This just proves it. You're castles, I'm cottages!"

The non sequitur sounded like the perfect segue into her calling their marriage a mistake again. The thought made a fire leap to life in his belly. But sucking in a quick breath, Trent clamped down on his sudden spike of temper. He thought he knew what was happening here, and she needed his patience.

Take it easy, Crosby. Don't let her get to you. "Rebecca—"

"Castles!" She, on the other hand, was working herself up into another mad. "Cottages!"

"But both cardboard," he pointed out, trying to derail her.

Her head whipped toward him. "What?"

"Castle or cottage, both are cardboard."

"I don't understand a thing you're saying." Tears wet her eyes again. "I don't understand what's happening to me," she whispered.

That got to him. Plunged straight into his chest. "Honey." Even though she tried to push him away, he pulled her into his arms. "It's hormones, sweetheart. Don't you think?"

She stilled. Sniffed. "Hormones?"

Her next sniff prompted Trent to pull his handkerchief from his back pocket and hand it over to her. "I took a look at that pregnancy book you've left lying around. It says you're likely to get emotional at unlikely moments over unlikely things."

"Emotional? At unlikely moments?" She looked up at him, hope in her damp eyes. "Do you suppose that's what it is?"

"Of course." God, if only all his problems could be solved so easily.

"Overemotional at unlikely moments over unlikely things." Rebecca appeared to mull that over, then her face broke into a beatific smile. "I feel *so* much better."

And so did he. As a matter of fact, her smile made him feel brilliant.

"I feel *so* relieved." Dropping his handkerchief, she knelt on the couch to take his face between her hands. "Hormones! For a few terrible moments I thought it was love." And then she kissed him.

A noisy, friendly kiss. But enough to distract him. Enough to take his mind off the word she'd said. It only came back to him when she leaned away again. *Love?* He grabbed her arm. "What did you say?"

"Love." Her face flushed, but she managed to meet his gaze. "Silly, huh? I shouldn't have mentioned it." As she looked away, it appeared she regretted it.

"Love?"

"I know, I know." She drew an intricate pattern on the fuzzy pink fabric of her nightwear. "It couldn't be, of course, because cardboard in common or not, you're a castle, I'm a cottage, and never the twain shall meet."

"That's a mixed metaphor, honey. And we not only met, but we married." But…love. *Hell.* Love. Why did it keep coming up?

Without stopping to consider what he was doing, though, he pulled Rebecca onto his lap. Without stopping to wonder why that one little word wouldn't stop echoing in his life and sounding in his head, he lowered his mouth to hers.

Love.

She was soft and warm and this kiss wasn't friendly. Yet he took her lips with tenderness, all the gentleness that he could come up with, because that word, that word *love,* sounded so pretty and so delicate when she said it.

When he came up for air, he looked down into her eyes and brushed the hair from her forehead. "And we're not castles or cottages, either. We're a man and a woman. So come on, Rebecca, let's make—"

Her fingers pressed against his mouth. "Hormones."

Let's make hormones?

"Please, Trent," she whispered.

Please let's make hormones, or please let's pretend with that word instead of the other? He took her hand away and kissed each fingertip. "I want you, Rebecca."

She swallowed. "I've slept alone all week, Trent. Why?"

He shook his head. "I've told myself a dozen reasons, none of which make the least bit of sense now that I have you in my arms."

"Then maybe we've both been wrong."

She meant she thought she'd been wrong about loving him. He closed his eyes. "Let's think about who has made what mistake later. Now let's—"

"Make hormones."

Whatever way she wanted to play it, it didn't matter. Once again, that other word was in his head and he couldn't seem to let it go. She'd said love. Love.

He opened his eyes. "How do you feel about this couch?" he asked. It was black leather and looked like something that should be in a psychiatrist's office.

She twisted her head to get a look at it, making him fascinated by the soft spot on her cheek beside her ear. He leaned forward to kiss it and felt her shiver.

"It's an ugly couch, Trent," she said. "Sorry."

"I think it's the color," he said, then kissed the corner of her mouth to distract her as he began sliding up the hem of her nightgown to draw it over her head. "It needs one that's softer."

He laid the empty pink garment on the leather expanse behind Rebecca. "It needs you." With his hands on her shoulders, he pushed her against the couch and followed her down.

Her thighs parted to make a place for him, and a hot tremor rolled over his skin. He rocked against her silky panties and, leaning on his elbows, filled his palms with her breasts.

Love.

The word was in his mind, in his mouth, on the tip of his tongue as he explored her body. He painted each letter on her naked chest. He breathed it against her belly button. When he pulled off her panties, it was in his palms as he ran them back up her bare inner thighs.

When he touched her between her legs, her little gasp sounded like something more than passion. More than hormones. She rocked into his fingers, giving herself to him, letting him learn more about her.

He leaned back down, spreading her thighs wider with his shoulders. She seemed to sense his intention and tried to scissor him away.

"Trent, I'm not sure..."

She wasn't sure she could open herself to him. Let him be so intimate with her. But that word was in the air and in her voice—*love*—and it pushed him to push her.

"Please, Rebecca," he said. He licked a path between her hipbones and cupped her breasts so that he could thumb her nipples. "Please, Rebecca."

Her breath was ragged. "You..."

"Yes, all for me." *Love.* He leaned down and nuzzled between her folds. "You, all for me." Her taste was sweet and womanly, and she cried out as he opened her for his kiss.

He explored her with his mouth, his heart pounding, his shaft aching with excitement. One of Rebecca's hands was in his hair and he reveled in the desperate bite of her nails against his scalp. "That's right," he whispered. "Give it to me." *Love.*

And as he felt her start to shake in climax, he kept tonguing her wet woman-flesh. Rebecca's flesh. As she moaned the sound of her release, he breathed out against her. *Love.* She climaxed again.

He undressed with one hand, keeping the other busy caressing her body. She watched him with languid eyes, her body sprawled against the ugly couch that would, from now on, forever be beautiful to him. "You make me feel selfish," she whispered.

"Selfish? You?" He laughed. "That's the last thing you are, sweetheart."

He crawled up her body to his favorite place between her legs. She played with his hair, then traced her fingers over his mouth. "You've got quite the technique, Mr. Crosby."

"I was inspired, Mrs. Crosby." *Love.*

Her legs wrapped around his waist, but he didn't enter her yet. This moment was too good to lose in the heat of sex. "Am I squishing you?"

Her hair swished against the leather as she shook her head. "Eisenhower isn't big enough yet."

"Eisenhower?" His eyes widened. "I thought you were leaning toward Matthew or Giselle."

"Inside joke." She stilled, laughed. "Really an inside joke." Her hand wandered to the back of his neck so she could pull him down for a kiss. "I like Trent," she said against his mouth.

"Trent Junior?"

There was a glint in her eye. "Trent Senior. You, I like."

Love. He didn't care what she had just said instead. Lifting his hips, he matched up their bodies. Later he'd think about why the word didn't scare the hell out of him. Later, he'd think about how one pretty little valentine had swept away all vestiges of his cynicism with one sweep of her eyelashes. How she'd washed his heart clean with her tears.

"This is for you, Rebecca," he said, entering her in a long, tender stroke. *Love.*

Her eyes drifted shut and her pelvis tipped into his to perfect the fit. "Aaah," they said together.

Her eyes opened and she gave him a smile with such power that he thought it could make a cottage into a castle, that it could cause a bitter skeptic like himself to be reborn. In a slow movement, he pulled himself out of her.

This is how it is when we're alone.

Then he sank in again, causing them both to shudder.

This is how it is when we're together.

Love.

A faster rhythm was impossible to deny himself. His body moved on its own, reaching for the pinnacle, while Trent's mind cataloged the details of the journey. Rebecca's flushed skin. Her swollen mouth. Her dark, dark eyes that blurred when he reached between them to touch her where they were joined.

"Trent?"

He felt a bead of sweat roll down his spine, the gathering of lust between his thighs. Pleasure was just out of reach, but Rebecca was right here. Rebecca...and love.

His body vaulted that last distance and his stroking fingers took Rebecca with him. They both cried out.

I love you.

It swirled around them. He could swear one of them had said it aloud.

And as beautiful as the moment was, as the feeling was, he hoped to God it wasn't him.

"I have something for you."

Rebecca turned at the sound of Trent's voice. Her eyes widened. Trent Crosby in black tie. The shorthand for that was…wow. Just *wow*.

As he approached, she plucked at the strapless slip she was wearing. Over it would go the new dress she had bought for the Summer Solstice dance at the country club. The slip was not revealing, at least not anymore than the dress itself, but with Trent moving toward her with that look in his eyes she felt naked.

Ever since that night on the couch in the den, every time he looked at her she felt equal parts excited and exposed. Her stomach jittered as he reached out to wrap his finger in one of her curls. "You're so pretty," he said.

She clamped down on the shiver that wanted to roll down her back. He was her husband, her lover, the father of her child. There was no reason for him to make her nervous.

Except that she'd said the *L*-word to him when she'd been complaining about the changes he'd made to the playhouse. It had popped out of her mouth, sprung by tears, sprung by Trent who'd been trying to help by reading her pregnancy books. *He read her pregnancy books.*

She felt herself tearing up at the thought.

"Sweetheart, what's wrong?" He ran his knuckle along her cheek.

"Mascara." She blinked in rapid succession to take care of the overflow moisture. To distract him, she touched her finger to his snowy shirtfront. "You said you had something for me."

He caught her hand and then drew it into the pocket of his jacket. A velvet box. A velvet jewelry box.

Her emotions did another dip and roll. "For me?" No one had ever given her a gift in a velvet jewelry box.

Men like Trent gave out jewelry.

"Aren't you going to take it out?" There was a smile in his eyes.

"Sure. Yes." So then she stood there like an idiot, holding the pale blue box in her palm.

"It won't bite, Rebecca." He leaned close, resting his forehead against hers. "Though I just might."

There was no way to control the next shiver. It skittered across her skin, raising goose bumps from her neck to her ankles. He had to be used to sophisticated women. Sophisticated women who had piles of jewelry from their lovers. Women who didn't shiver at the word *bite*. Women who didn't imagine the man in their bed whispered "I love you" every time they had sex.

Loving Trent made her feel inadequate and elated by turns. She'd tried to cover for her slip about love by latching on to the whole hormones thing, but while she hoped she'd fooled Trent, she'd never once fooled herself.

She loved him. She was in love with him.

Since that night, though, he'd never mentioned the word again.

"Open it now, honey. I'll help you get it on, then I have to leave." He tipped up her chin with his finger. "Don't be too far behind."

They were taking separate cars because he had an errand and some extra duties as the club's membership chair. She'd opted for getting ready at a more leisurely pace and driving herself. Taking a deep breath, Rebecca flipped open the box. She looked at the necklace inside and then looked up at Trent, puzzled.

"This doesn't look like something you'd choose." She'd didn't know quite what she'd expected, but this wasn't big or flashy.

He shrugged. "It looks like something you'd wear."

Rebecca bent her head for a closer inspection. It was a delicate chain, platinum she assumed, and hanging from it was a little—

"Angel," she said, lifting it with her finger. A tiny angel, its round head, triangle body, and wings created with frames of more platinum, like stained glass. But between the platinum lines, instead of glass, were jewels. Clear jewels.

"Diamonds," Trent said. "But check out the halo. That's my favorite part."

A platinum squiggle circled the angel's diamond head. She glanced at Trent again.

"Can you see the letter the halo makes?"

Rebecca lifted the necklace out of the box and held

it against her palm. "It's an *E*," she said. The halo was in the shape of a cursive *E*."

He smiled and ran the back of his finger down her cheek. "For Eisenhower."

"Oh." Her eyes filled with tears again.

Trent laughed. "You're going to make me think you don't like my gift."

"I *love* your gift."

Love. The word seemed to glow like neon letters between them.

"Rebecca…"

She turned her back on the unreadable expression in his eyes. "Put the necklace on for me, please," she said.

He fastened the necklace. "There."

She spun to look at her reflection instead of him. "It's beautiful, Trent," she said. Her gaze met his in the mirror. "Thank you. Really."

He grinned. "You're welcome. Really." Then he checked his watch. "I'd better go. I can't wait to see you and the new dress at the club."

"And Angel Eisenhower," Rebecca added, touching the necklace, then going on tiptoe to lightly kiss his mouth.

Trent covered her belly with his palm. He'd never done that before, touched her quite like that, as though he was touching their baby. She swallowed hard.

"And Angel Eisenhower," he confirmed. And then he was gone.

As she pulled her dress from the closet, she noticed a small ache in her lower back. "Stupid high heels," she muttered, staring down at the strappy sandals on her feet. They were hard to get used to for a woman accustomed to flat-soled, comfortable nurse shoes. But she supposed flat-soled, comfortable nurse shoes would look pretty ridiculous with the turquoise-colored, tissue-fine silk dress she'd bought.

Trent was used to women who could wear sophisticated shoes with their sophisticated dresses at their fancy country-club dances.

As she wiggled into the dress and it settled into place, her lower back twinged again. She ignored it as she inspected herself in the mirror. The fabric clung to her pregnancy-enhanced breasts, but skimmed the rest of her figure. The hemline fell to the ground at the back, but lifted over one leg, almost to mini-height. When she walked, in the front it showed a lot of the legs that Trent claimed to adore. In the back, the dress frothed in a shape she found pretty. She hoped he found it sophisticated and the right choice for the Solstice dance.

On the other side of the room the phone rang. Rebecca glanced at it, glanced back for a final inspection. "Because I don't want to let Trent down," she told her reflection.

Twelve

But letting Trent down weighed heavily on Rebecca's mind as she hurried into the Tanglewood Country Club and toward the sound of a live band playing something soft and dreamy in the reception hall/ballroom that was opposite the entrance to the restaurant. The phone call she'd received right after putting on her new dress had been from the hospital. Merry had been admitted again and was asking for Nurse Rebecca.

Even though Trent—reached by cell phone—had encouraged her to visit the child on her way to the dance, she'd had to wait for Merry to be settled in her room, further delaying Rebecca. As the minutes ticked away she'd felt tension turning those twinging aches in her lower back to tight knots. Tonight's dance was to be hers and Trent's first appearance as a couple at a country-club social occasion and she knew the evening was important to him.

Reaching the open double doors, she paused to catch her breath. The room looked beautiful, the chandeliers dimmed in favor of strings of hundreds of fairy lights. White flowers decorated the tables and topiary trees of white roses lined the walls. Magical, she couldn't help thinking.

She smiled to herself. Who would have thought that what they'd gone into for practical reasons could have turned her so idealistic about romance and love?

Who would have thought a navy-brat-turned-nurse would be poised at the entrance to Portland's most exclusive country club, seeking out her sexy, handsome and—at least in her imagination, anyway—loving husband?

Remembering once again she was late, she took a few hurried steps inside the dimly lit room. A wave of hot, humid air struck her in the face. Another pang, stronger than any before, centered in her lower back, and more heat washed down her skin. Feeling almost sick from the combination, she stopped again, scanning the room for Trent and hoping their table was close by.

In the crowd of dark jackets she couldn't seem to make him out. The fairy lights twinkled, then blurred. She blinked, trying to clear her vision. Glassware clattered so loudly in her ears that it drowned out the music of the band. The couples on the dance floor didn't appear affected, though. They moved smoothly about, beautiful women and handsome men.

Trent.

The muscles in her lower back pinched harshly again as she recognized him. A tall woman was in his arms, a stunning blonde in a sequined dress whose diamond collar was as different from Rebecca's simple angel necklace as the woman was different from Rebecca herself.

But still, Trent was *her* husband. The father of her child. Pressing a hand over her belly button she took a deep breath and then threaded her way through the tables toward him. She'd catch his eye while he danced and have him direct her to her seat.

The room was a thousand miles long. In her ridiculous shoes she could only take small steps. But she kept her eyes on the prize, on Trent, thinking she'd feel better when she made contact with him. She wouldn't be so hot, her back wouldn't ache so and she would hear the music instead of the cacophony of background noises that were clanging in her head.

A cold hand grazed her arm.

Rebecca looked down, blinking at the woman who was touching her. The fairy lights seemed to be doing more than twinkling now; they seemed to be moving around the room like fireflies. She blinked again, trying to make them still.

"You must be Trent's wife," the stranger said.

Rebecca could barely hear the words over the loud sounds in her head. "Yes," she said. If only those lights would stay still! "How did you know?"

"I've been watching for you, and you were watching him."

Rebecca glanced over at the dance floor again. There was Trent, his dark blond head bent low to his partner's champagne-colored hair. Rebecca had danced with him once, too, she thought, but not as well as he danced with the woman he was with now. Her stomach went queasy.

"I'm Trent's mother, Sheila Crosby."

His mother? Trying to pull herself together, Rebecca pasted on a smile. "How do you do? I'm Rebecca Holley."

Sheila Crosby cocked an eyebrow. She was another beautiful woman, another in the mold of the one Trent now held in his arms. Blond, toned, face and hair model-perfect.

"You kept your own last name?" Sheila asked.

The room was starting to spin. What had Trent's mother said? Something about using her own last name? "No," Rebecca replied, wondering how anyone could think in the cloying heat of the room. "I— No. I guess I made a mistake."

Sheila laughed and cast a pointed glance toward something or someone Rebecca couldn't see. "Marrying a Crosby is always a mistake."

And she should respond to that how? Her back muscles were tightening into a ruthless, relentless ache. She had to get these shoes off. She had to cool herself down with a glass of water. Trying another smile, Rebecca began edging away. "It was nice meeting you. I'm sure we'll see each other again."

"Not if my son has any say about it."

Rebecca kept moving, trying to think through the too-sharp sounds still clamoring in her skull. Did Trent's mother think he was ashamed of Rebecca? That he wanted to distance himself and his family from her? But no, that wasn't right. She'd spent time with his sister. Had met his father earlier in the week.

Trent had wanted her at his side tonight, even though now he was dancing with someone else. At the thought, her back muscles cramped again, tighter than before. She gasped, trying to ride out the pain.

"Miss? Are you all right?"

A man's voice now. A man in a tuxedo, but black-haired, black-eyed. Not Trent.

"Fine," Rebecca managed to get out. She needed to find Trent, but darkness was closing in on her vision. The fairy lights were dancing about the room. Trent was somewhere, dancing, too, with a woman who was so much more than Rebecca...except the mother of his child.

Her lower back spasmed again, and this time the pain wrapped around her pelvis and squeezed. Rebecca reached out and grabbed the strange man at her side as the pain cinched tight and a liquid sensation trickled between her legs.

It was as if she'd started her period, Rebecca thought, still clutching the stranger. But that couldn't be right. She was pregnant with Eisenhower. Another cramp closed down on her womb.

She was pregnant with Eisenhower!

Another trickle.

As a cold sweat broke out over her skin, Rebecca called out, "Trent! Trent!" Her gaze searched him out. "Trent!"

Then she located him. He was still on the dance floor, but now he broke away from the beauty who was so much more than Rebecca...except the mother of his child.

But when another cramp seized her body, a horrible dread seized her too.

Perhaps she wasn't going to be the mother of Trent's child, after all.

Trent was good in a crisis. Everyone had always said so. Everyone said it at the club tonight. They praised his calm as he moved toward the pale and trembling Rebecca, as he moved her out of the room, as he handed his keys to the valet and waited for his car to be brought around.

"You're going to be all right, sweetheart." He settled her quickly into the passenger seat, angling its back to a recline and then wrapping his jacket snugly around her body. "Are you certain we don't need an ambulance?"

"We don't need an ambulance."

Above his black coat, her face was a pale smudge. The sight clawed at his gut. She'd had stars shining in her eyes when he'd left her tonight and now he felt as if all the stars had fallen from the sky. "The hospital—"

"No. We don't need that either. The bleeding has already stopped. The doctor said to go home and put my feet up. This might be nothing. The only thing to do at the moment is wait."

Trent slid into his own seat and then gripped the steering wheel. Problem was, though he was good in a crisis, he wasn't so good at waiting. He started the car and pulled smoothly away from the curb, focusing on not jostling Rebecca any more than necessary.

He glanced over, noting that she'd closed her eyes. If waiting was what it took, then he was going to be the best, most cheerful, patient, helpful, supportive waiter in the whole damn world. He could do this. His poker face had served him well in dozens of negotiations and it would serve him well now.

Keeping it together would only help them both.

"It won't be long," Rebecca said.

"What, sweetheart?" He sounded normal. Almost relaxed. Amazing. "What won't be long?"

She shook her head and he saw a single tear leak from beneath her lashes. "Everything," she said in a tired voice. "All of it ends too soon."

What the hell does she mean by that? But a car cut in front of him and he had to give his attention to making a tricky maneuver into the next lane. When he had a second to glance at Rebecca again, she appeared asleep.

Good. Rest, my love. His jacket had slipped, revealing her neck and one shoulder. He saw that her hand lay across one breast, her fingers holding fast to the angel he'd given her.

Over the next hours, Trent learned a lot about his wife.

She was as calm in a crisis as he was.

Her unfailing politeness unnerved him.

Her self-reliance unnerved him.

Her silence unnerved him, especially when she said she was going to sleep and he knew it was all a sham, that she was lying beside him on the mattress, awake and quiet.

So damn quiet.

At 3:00 a.m., conceding a momentary defeat, he cursed and flipped on the bedside light. It surprised her into blinking at him.

"I'd say I was sorry I woke you," he said, "but I know you weren't asleep."

She pushed her hair away from her face to look at him. That was all that she did. She just looked at him. Calmly.

He found that damn unnerving, too. He wanted her to talk, wail, yell, show some kind of emotion, *share* her emotion with him. "It's going to be okay," he said when he couldn't stand the silence any longer.

She shook her head.

"What do you mean?" There was the tiniest hint of strain in his voice, so he cleared his throat to wipe it away. He was great in a crisis, damn it, and it was up to him to keep things together.

"Turn off the light, Trent." She turned her head away from him. "Please. Turn off the light and let me sleep."

What could he do but obey? It was a rational man's move, and he was always rational. And right. Everything *was* going to be okay.

Sometime before dawn he fell asleep. When he woke up, it was after seven and he was alone in the bed. The adjoining bathroom door clicked open and his gaze jumped to Rebecca.

She slowly emerged, her hair brushed, her face looking freshly washed. He noted she was still in the flannel nightgown she'd dressed in the night before.

But now, in the notch of the neckline, he could see that the little angel she'd worn to bed the night before was gone.

In the waiting room at the OB/GYN's office, they gave Trent a pamphlet to read. Though he kept his face impassive, the unknowns pissed him off. The medical profession, all those experts and researchers and M.D.s and Ph.D.s didn't know exactly how many pregnant women had miscarriages in the first twenty weeks of pregnancy, though they thought somewhere around twenty-five percent. Usually it occurred before the thirteenth week—Rebecca had been in her eleventh—but they didn't fully understand the causes, except to know that it wasn't brought on by work, exercise or sex.

What they *did* know was that in most cases a woman would go on to have a normal pregnancy—and that couples could start trying again in a couple of months. What they *did* know was that a couple, especially a woman, might feel some level of loss.

What nobody knew but Trent was Rebecca's reasons for wanting the child they'd lost. She'd told him that she'd wanted a child to fill her well, a child to repair her heart that was broken a little bit by her job every day. How empty would this make her feel? How heart-broken?

His fingers tightened on the pamphlet, creasing the businesslike buff paper. He wanted to crush it, slam it to the floor, grind it into the gruesome green carpeting with his heel. But he was the type of man who controlled his emotions, right? And then Rebecca chose that moment to emerge from the door that led to the examining rooms.

Jumping to his feet, he searched her pallid face while making sure his was completely impassive. "All set?"

"I need to check in at the hospital. There's a…procedure."

"A procedure?" He leaped toward her.

She held up her hand. "Nothing major. No big deal. Just a simple procedure to make sure that…that…"

Okay, okay. He'd read about that, too. A common procedure to make sure there was nothing the miscarried pregnancy might have left behind. It wasn't something to get worked up about. He made himself calmly nod. "All right. Well, let's take care of it, shall we?"

And just like that, his wife was admitted to the hospital for a surgical procedure that required him to sign papers and releases and read warnings that set his heart thumping and his stomach churning. But revealing that wouldn't help Rebecca at all, so he examined them with care and signed them without showing any hint of what he was feeling.

As a matter of fact, he wasn't sure if he felt anything at all. He kept going numb, and he welcomed it.

It helped him as he watched her being wheeled off on a gurney and then again as he went about accomplishing the practical tasks that had to be done next. They were going to keep Rebecca overnight, so in the hospital gift shop he bought her three nightgowns, two robes and two pairs of slippers. That way she'd have choices. He also bought ten glossy magazines, a bag of candy bars, a bear holding a bouquet of balloons, a bear holding a bouquet of flowers, a bear holding a bouquet of suckers. Then he thought the bears might remind her too much of the baby, so he dropped them off on the pediatric floor and started all over again.

One single, silver balloon with a star on it.

A flowering orchid plant, whose creamy petals reminded him of Rebecca's skin.

Five pounds of solid chocolate carved in the shape of a golf ball sitting on a tee.

Then it was all about waiting again.

He didn't last five minutes. At a nearby pay phone— a cranky nurse told him his cell phone was *verboten*— he called Katie at the Crosby Systems offices.

"Where the heck *are* you?" she demanded.

He went the cool, rational route with her, too. He'd called Claudine about the miscarriage, so his sister knew about that. Now he offered up the facts about Rebecca's stay in the hospital.

"Oh, Trent." Katie's voice, full of sympathy, made him rub at his chest.

"It's going to be fine," he said. *Think numb. Numb was good.* "Everything's going to be fine."

"Really?" There was a break in his little sister's voice.

"Sure. Of course." His entire life he'd kept it together for Katie. Took care of her when their mother wouldn't. Wiped her nose, bandaged her hurts, didn't let himself appear vulnerable in case it would scare her. He'd done the same thing for Ivy and he was going to keep to that program now.

"You'll call me back if you or Rebecca need anything?"

"Sure I will."

When he hung up, the hands of the clock on the waiting room wall had slowed to a snail's pace. So he called his brother Danny.

"Just checking in," he said when he heard his brother's voice on the other end of the line.

"You okay?" Danny asked.

"Of course. Are *you?*"

A sigh sounded. "Trent, I just hung up with Katie. I know how things are."

"Then you know that I can handle them." Though he was glad to hear his brother's voice, it was Trent who had always looked after Danny, too. When he'd been miserable at the military school their parents had sent him to, it was Trent who had insisted their father remove him. When Danny had fallen into the gutter of drugs and alcohol, it was Trent who had pulled him out and brought him back to life and back into the family business.

"You can handle anything," Danny agreed.

Certain the assertion would settle him down, Trent

ended the call. The chairs were hellishly uncomfort-
able, so he remained standing. His legs had the jitters
so he paced. He tried reading an old issue of *Business-
Week,* but even an article he'd missed on the CEOs to
watch in the twenty-first century—he was mentioned—
couldn't keep his interest.

He went to the phone again. This time when he heard
his brother's hello, the facade he'd been keeping, for
maybe as long as forever, cracked. "I have a problem,"
he heard himself say.

"Who is this?" Danny replied.

"Your brother, for God's sake. I have a problem and
I don't know what to do next."

There was a long silence on the other end of the line.

"Danny, are you there?"

"Sorry, first I was pinching myself and then I was
considering exactly how to determine if hell has truly
frozen over."

"Very funny."

The humor in Danny's voice dried up. "I know it's
not, Trent. It's just that you've been wearing your superhero cape for so long that it's strange to see you
without it."

"Superhero. Give me a break."

"We never did, did we?" Danny countered. "Not Mom,
not me, not our sisters, not Dad when he handed all the
headaches over to you, whether it was the responsibility
for your siblings or the responsibility for Crosby
Systems."

Trent frowned. "I'm damn good with all that."

"Yeah. So what aren't you good at?"

"Rebecca." That word spilled from his mouth, and then more. "Maybe I made a mistake with Rebecca."

"First a problem, and now you're admitting to making a *mistake?*" Danny laughed. "I can't believe it."

"I said *maybe*. And why the hell are you laughing harder now? For the first time in our lives I'm calling you for help and you're amused." He took a breath. "I'm afraid, Danny. I'm afraid I'll lose Rebecca."

"Hell, Trent." Danny's voice turned gruff with the emotion of having lost both son and wife himself. "She's in good hands at Portland General, right?"

Trent closed his eyes, squeezing them tightly. "I think she'll be fine physically. But I'm scared that after this she'll leave me."

It was out. And the fear wasn't any prettier or easier under the harsh fluorescent lights.

"Don't let her," Danny said hoarsely. "Hang on tight. Hit her with whatever you can to keep her beside you. Never give up."

Trent rocked back on his heels. "Crosbys never give up."

"No, they don't." And the certainty in his brother's voice told Trent that he was thinking of Noah, who'd been gone for four long years but who lived every day in his brother's heart. Then Danny gave one last piece of advice. "Call Katie. Tell her everything you've told me."

Trent surprised himself by doing that very thing. And then, in the blink of an eye, it seemed, he was bemused to find her at his side, plying him with coffee and a sandwich. Rubbing a hand over his face, he tried to figure out if Katie was really there in the waiting room or if he'd dreamed her up.

"What are you doing here?" he said. The coffee felt hot. The sandwich was pastrami, his favorite.

"Taking care of you, for once."

"Oh-kay."

"And dispensing my best piece of advice in person."

He narrowed his eyes at her. "What's that?"

"If you want to keep Rebecca in your life, Trent, you've got to tell her the truth. You've got to take that big risk, big brother, and tell her you're in love with her."

He pretended the idea didn't plunge an icy, sharp claw through all that convenient numbness he'd been experiencing. "How do you know I haven't?"

His little sister snorted. "There's a stupid question. I know because, Trent, I know *you*."

Thirteen

Lying on her side on a bed, Rebecca awoke, but kept her eyes shut. It was night. Not that she could see through her eyelids. But she could feel it. She could hear it in the hush of the hallway outside the door of her hospital room.

Hospitals were busy places that muffled the noise of their bustle as well as they could in the evening hours, but it was a muffle that Rebecca knew well. Staying overnight hadn't been necessary, of course. But her friends on the hospital staff had insisted, and she'd been so preoccupied with other thoughts that she'd agreed without protest.

She'd miscarried the baby.

Thinking it yet again, her legs automatically drew up

toward her chest, as if to protect the life growing inside her. But it was too late.

"Rebecca?" a female voice said softly. "Are you awake?"

A nurse coming in to take her blood pressure or her temperature, she thought. She let her eyes drift open.

Instead of a co-worker, it was Katie Logan who had spoken from one of two chairs pulled up near the bed. Beside her sat Trent.

"Yes, I'm awake," Rebecca said, speaking to them both. Trent was wearing the same clothes he'd been in when he'd taken her to the doctor's office—slacks, a dress shirt, no tie, a sports jacket. There was the slightest hint of whiskers along his chin, but other than that he appeared impeccable, as always. "What time is it?"

His gaze not leaving her face, he shrugged.

Katie turned her wrist to check her watch. "Nearing eleven. I should get going, but I wanted to talk to you before I left."

Rebecca blinked. "Did you need something?"

Katie shook her head. "No, no. I only wanted to tell you how sorry both Peter and I are and to ask if *you* needed something." Tears sprang into her eyes and she shot Trent a guilty glance. "I'm not getting weepy. He hates weepy."

"I don't need anything, Katie." *Except my baby back.* "But thank you very much for asking."

The other woman reached over to pat Rebecca's hand. "I—" She broke off with an audible sniff.

"Say goodbye, Katie," Trent put in, his voice calm

but implacable. "We don't want to have to call in flood control."

His sister made a face. "Goodbye, Katie," she parroted. Then she leaned over to kiss Rebecca's cheek. "Goodbye, Rebecca."

The other woman's belly looked round and healthy and beautiful. Rebecca couldn't take her eyes off it, and wondered if the signs of someone else's pregnancy would always stab her in the heart. But she managed a smile. "Goodbye, Katie. And thank you again."

That left her alone with Trent. She took in a long breath, then let it go. "I didn't expect you to be here."

"Where did you expect me to be?" Leaning forward, he propped his elbows on his knees and rested his linked hands on the mattress.

She shrugged, her gaze fixed on his fingers. They were long, slightly tanned. There were calluses on their undersides from the grip of his racquetball racket, she knew. They added a masculine roughness to even the most gentle caress. His nails were clipped close, and for the first time she noticed that the knuckles of his right hand were scarred.

With the tip of her forefinger, Rebecca touched one. "How did you get these scars?"

He didn't bother looking at them. "Punched a wall."

Her gaze flew to his face. "You?" Punching walls seemed a bit hotheaded for Trent Crosby, Mr. In Control, the invulnerable businessman.

"It was after Danny's wife died."

The words were said with dispassion. But how he'd

behaved after his sister-in-law's suicide—Rebecca remembered that—suggested that Trent had been filled
with fierce emotion. That Trent could feel fierce emotion was something she'd never seen from him, though.
"That must have been a difficult time."

"Yeah." He straightened in the chair. "But enough
about that. How are you feeling?"

"Fine."

He cocked a brow.

"Tired. But nothing hurts, if that's what you mean."

His mouth opened as if he was about to say something, then it closed. With an odd little movement, he
gestured toward the wheeled table beside the bed. "People have brought things."

"Oh." She leaned up on an elbow and pulled the
table closer. There was an immense bouquet from the
OR and some smaller arrangements from Rebecca's
closer friends on the staff. "I suppose the news about
the miscarriage is all over the hospital by now."

"Yes."

The way he said the word had her staring at him
again. She caught a new expression on his face—
actually his first expression. Ever since she'd told him
about the miscarriage that morning he'd been so non-
committal. Good Lord, had it only been that morning?
It seemed like a lifetime ago.

Eisenhower's lifetime.

Her heart squeezed, raining sadness like a squeezed
sponge. Rebecca dropped back against the pillows, her
head clogging with tears.

He hates weepy, Katie had said.

Rebecca closed her eyes so Trent wouldn't know how close to weepy she was.

He cleared his throat. "I brought you some things, too. Nightgowns and such. Katie put them in the little closet over there. But the orchid plant is from me and the silver balloon and the chocolate golf ball."

A chocolate golf ball? She opened her eyes and looked at Trent again, surprised once more by that funny expression on his face. It was as if he was awkward or uncertain or…

Sad.

She hadn't been thinking that losing the baby was his loss as well. But he'd been so stoic through the whole thing, since last night when she'd called his name in such a panic at the dance, that she hadn't thought about what he might be feeling.

What *was* he feeling?

As if to avoid her gaze, he started fiddling with the controls that powered the wall-mounted television and the bed.

Maybe they should share their thoughts with each other. Maybe that would make them both feel better. Maybe that would make her not feel so alone.

The television suddenly clicked on. Both she and Trent turned to it automatically. "In local developments," the newscaster said. "Everett Baker, held without bail on charges that range from burglary to kidnapping in relation to the Sanders case and others, fired his public defender today. He's pleading guilty to all counts."

Everett Baker. All counts.

A chill walked down her spine.

Rebecca had rarely thought of Everett Baker since that night that she and Trent had eaten dinner at Katie and Peter's. That night when Trent had whispered to her, *Let's make a baby.* She'd let herself believe that night they had.

But now she remembered. Now she had to face the truth, didn't she? She had been pregnant with Trent's baby because of a malicious prank. Trent hadn't wanted a child, he hadn't wanted Rebecca.

They'd both been foisted on him, thrust into his life.

The emotion she'd just glimpsed on his face was probably relief. He didn't have to be saddled with navy-brat Nurse Rebecca any longer. Tears of self-pity stung the corners of her eyes again.

He would have made a fine father. She knew that. But the fact was, there was no baby any longer.

And no reason for Trent to be married to her.

Everett Baker had slept well the night before. Slept well for the first time in months. Maybe years.

Maybe since he was six years old.

When the guard delivered his breakfast, he thanked the man and then he asked him to pass along his request to those detectives working his case. "Tell them I want to talk. Tell them I have even more they need to know."

As he'd suspected, it didn't take long for the guards to move him into an interview room. It wasn't dingy like the ones they showed on his favorite TV show, both in prime time and reruns—*Law & Order.* It was freshly painted; the plastic table's top had a woodgrain finish. The chairs were cushioned. The detectives weren't anything like Lenny or Ray or the LT on *Law & Order,* either. They didn't exchange any fast-paced dialogue, and there weren't any witty one-liners.

In the past weeks, Everett had learned that being held for his crimes was nothing like watching an episode from the show, either. Of course, committing the crimes themselves was nothing like TV had prepared him for, though sometimes he had pictured himself as a character in a story while carrying them out. It made it easier to think of it as someone else breaking the laws.

Not Everett Baker.

Which made sense, when he thought about it. He looked up as two men settled into chairs across the table from him.

One was Detective Abe Levine, from the Portland Police Department, the man he'd called when he'd decided to turn himself in. The detective was average height, stocky, with salt-and-pepper hair. His nose looked as broken-in as his rumpled suit. The other man with him was FBI Agent Drew Delane. He had sharp features, a sharply pressed black suit, a sharp way of speaking.

Everett clasped his hands on the table in front of him and decided to get it out as quickly as he could. "Everett Baker isn't my real name."

The two men glanced at each other. "What?" Detective Levine said. "We ran a check on you, Everett. You have a social security number, a driver's license. There are high-school and college transcripts, *your* transcripts. I saw the attached photos myself."

"I know." Everett nodded. "Let me start from the beginning, all right?"

The men shared another look. "Finally. You're going to tell us everything?"

"Yes, I'm going to tell you it all."

"Why now, Mr. Baker?" Agent Delane didn't go in for first names. He was the most hard-nosed of all those in authority whom Everett had spoken with since he'd confessed.

"Nancy," he answered. She'd visited him the day before and now when he said her name, he could see her face, her kind hazel eyes framed by a fringe of brown bangs. He could hear her laugh. He remembered how from the beginning she had reached through the barrier of his shyness with her friendly warmth. And then, later, with her generous passion.

"We told you, Everett," Levine said, "we're not charging her with anything."

Agent Delane didn't blink. "But we might."

Everett sent Detective Levine a grateful smile and ignored the FBI agent. "I'm telling the whole story because Nancy makes me believe that good might come out of the truth. That maybe I'm not solely to blame for all that happened."

Crossing his arms over his chest, Agent Delane lifted a brow. "So who *is* to blame, Mr. Baker?"

Mr. Baker, of course. But such an answer would only confuse them. Everett opened his mouth, ready to start from the beginning as he'd said, but then found himself stalled again. It was hard to say aloud. So hard to conquer his shame and his sadness.

"Mr. Baker, don't play games with us. What is this new information you want us to know?"

"It's about…about…Charlie Prescott." Okay, it wasn't the beginning, but it was a place to start.

He explained to them how he'd met the other man. When he'd moved to Portland and landed the job at Children's Connection, he'd hadn't known anyone in the city. "I found a local place, The Pub. It's nothing fancy or hip, but I'd go there for a drink and a cheap meal nearly every night. That's where I met Charlie."

"Yeah, yeah, yeah," Agent Delane said impatiently. "We know about Prescott's involvement from the computer files and phone records. We know that over a couple of drinks, the two of you decided to go into the baby-stealing business."

Everett pushed his hair off his forehead. "That's what I've been thinking about, all day, every day in my cell. I've been trying to think how this happened, how I got into this mess, step-by-step, following the trail backward. I'm trained as an accountant, and I think I finally see how it all adds up."

"And how is that?"

"I—I always wanted money. That accountant thing again, right? We moved around a lot when I was a kid. The people who raised me drank their paychecks if they had any jobs at all. The security of a stockpile of extra cash appealed to me."

Agent Delane narrowed his eyes and his voice filled with disgust. "So, hey, why not take someone else's kid?"

It sounded sick the way he said it. It made Everett sick to think of it. "I remember telling Charlie about the black market for babies. I'd overheard a couple of social workers in the cafeteria talking about how it worked. He latched on to the idea and kept bringing it up every night. How we'd be doing nothing different than what Children's Connection did—giving kids a home. Just different homes. And we'd profit instead of Children's Connection."

Everett pushed his hair away again. "The more he brought it up, the more I started to drink. Charlie was buying."

"If it was really all Charlie Prescott's idea, why didn't you walk away from him, Everett?"

Staring down at the table, he shook his head. It was so hard to explain and he was so deeply ashamed. "Because…because finally I had a friend. I was lonely in Portland, I don't join groups easily, and Charlie seemed to like me. Then, the more we talked about the black-market scheme, the more it started to make sense. A twisted sense, I see that now. But Charlie started calling himself the Stork and telling me how we'd profit from the babies. We saw ourselves as a pair of entrepreneurs on the road to riches."

It sounded sordid and pitiful when he said it aloud. But he forced himself through it, telling the men how Charlie and Vladimir Kosanisky had set up the Russian side of the scheme.

"Bad went to worse when I met Nancy. When I started spending time with her." But by that time, Nancy had become his salvation. It was her sweetness, her goodness, that had shown what a contrast to that *he* was. "Charlie was worried I'd confess to her what were doing." He transferred his gaze to Detective Levine. "Even Charlie could tell right away that Nancy would never go along with our scheme or even look the other way."

Then Charlie had outlined the next phase of his plan—stealing American babies from poor mothers and selling them to the wealthy. "After the first abduction, I told Charlie I wouldn't do it anymore. But he threatened to tell Nancy about our crimes. I knew she'd hate me if she found out, and worse, hate herself for being involved with someone like me."

But she'd proven her mettle once again. When Everett had told her everything, she'd cried. But she'd cried for them both.

"So where does the shell game with the sperm vials come in?"

Everett flushed. "That was all Charlie's idea. It wasn't about money. That's what I don't know—why Charlie went after Children's Connection from that angle."

Agent Delane looked skeptical again. "So it was just another of Charlie's ideas?"

Everett met his gaze. "Yes. He seemed determined to tarnish the clinic's reputation in every way he could."

"Well, Everett, you sure make yourself out to be the

lesser of two evils." There was more than a hint of a sneer in Agent Delane's voice. "Maybe Nancy's right about you."

She should hate him. But she didn't. It was that goodness in her, that goodness that she said she saw in *him,* that had made him want to atone for all his misdeeds. If Nancy, the woman he loved, thought he was worth something, then by God he was going to prove she was right.

Detective Levine licked his finger and paged back through his notes. "But wait. You said your name isn't Everett Baker. What's that about?"

That was the irony, the agony, the essence of it all. "Before the woman who made me call her Mom died, she told me something that put together puzzling memories and fears I'd had for as long as I could remember. She told me that her husband had kidnapped me when I was six years old. There was a scrapbook of clippings she had about the case. When she showed it to me, I believed her. That's why I moved to Portland after she was gone. I wanted to…come home."

To at least be close to the family he had failed. How could he have forgotten them? How could he have lost the faith so easily?

The men on the other side of the table were staring at him and frowning. "Who the hell are you really, Everett?" Detective Levine demanded.

"Robbie." At the sound of the name, the memories he'd retained flickered to life. Opening a Christmas gift. A baseball game, with a man's hand passing him a hot dog. It was the best hot dog he'd ever tasted in his life, he remembered that. His memory of his mother was only a smell, a perfume that he could never forget because it seemed to have cookies and blankets and flowers all wrapped up within it. There were others, and they'd finally made sense to him once he'd learned his true identity.

He looked up at the two other men. "My real name is Robbie Logan."

Rebecca had fallen asleep shortly after the eleven o'clock news, and, not knowing what to do with himself, Trent had gone home. Maybe he should have stayed with her at the hospital, but she'd gazed on him with such sadness that he'd decided to give her some space. Perhaps looking at her husband made her only more despondent about her lost baby.

Of course he hadn't told her he loved her. It seemed too risky when she was so shadow-eyed and quiet. So he'd stuffed all his emotions deeper inside himself, as far as they could go, in order to provide for her what she needed most. Someone calm. Rational. Reasonable. Logical.

But that was yesterday. After a sleepless night, Trent was rushing back to the hospital. Danny had told him to stick close to her. Katie had advised him to tell her he loved her.

He'd done neither, and the pale-rose dawn had told him that might be the biggest mistake of all.

It was sometime before 7:00 a.m. as he hurried down the hall to Rebecca's room. He hoped to find her still asleep so that when she opened her eyes he'd be right where he'd been the night before. Then he'd tell her how much she meant to him. Then he'd do what he had to do to keep her close.

The door to her room was open.

A murmur of voices drifted out of it.

She wasn't alone, he thought, pausing just outside. He looked in. She wasn't asleep, either.

She was fully dressed and surrounded by a knot of nurses.

In the midst of them, Rebecca was still Rebecca. Instead of playing patient, she was doing for others. Asking one woman about her husband. Asking another about their favorite patient, Merry. All with a sewing needle in her hand, as she repaired the pocket on the smock of a third woman.

How could he have ever labeled any woman "selfish" when knowing Rebecca swept away all sweeping generalizations?

In his chest, his heart moved. No, it grew, making it hard for him to breathe. "Rebecca." His voice came out hoarse.

She looked up. There were still shadows beneath her big Bambi eyes. He hated those shadows.

One of the other nurses smiled at him. "There's your handsome husband, Rebecca. You have him take you home and pamper you. Only Chinese food and hot fudge sundaes for the next week. Seven days of that and I guarantee the blues will be banished."

Rebecca half smiled, looking less-than-half convinced. "Don't let the staff nutritionist hear that prescription, Donna."

"Just give yourself time, honey," Donna said, then gestured to include the two other nurses. "Remember that the three of us have been through it."

"The four of us," Rebecca added.

Donna nodded toward Trent. "Make that five, right?"

Rebecca said nothing.

The other women started moving for the door. Trent stepped aside to let them pass. One patted his arm, one patted his cheek, one squeezed his hand. Nurses were touchy-feely people, all of them.

He headed toward Rebecca, but this particular touchy-feely nurse stiffened as he neared, and leaped away from the bed. Her flowers and gifts sat in two cardboard boxes on the mattress.

Her obvious tension put him off his game again. He cleared his throat. "Did the doctor come by? Is there anything new?"

She shook her head. "He only reiterated what he said yesterday. There's nothing physical about me to account for the…the loss." Her gaze flicked to his face, flicked away. "He said it was no problem. That I'll be able to have another child."

Trent's heart made the painful expansion again. Damn that doctor. That had been the wrong thing to say to Rebecca. He could see how wrong it had been, clear as day, by the bleak expression on her face.

No problem. Another child.

His heart was choking him again.

Hadn't he always known the damn things—hearts—were an inconvenience, if not out-and-out dangerous? He swallowed, stuffing everything back down inside again.

It was no time to get sentimental. It was time to be strong for Rebecca and get her back home where she belonged.

Fourteen

Relief rushed through Rebecca as she walked into Trent's house. Not because the place felt homey, but here were her clothes, her books, her keys. Here she could pick up her life and move on with it.

Another base posting. Think of it as just another base posting.

"Everything okay?" Trent asked.

She realized she was standing in the foyer, staring at the arrangement on the dining room table. As usual, the fresh flowers were tortured into a stiff and spiky arrangement. In the past she would have released the gladiolus and Queen Anne's lace from their formal prison, setting them free to arch and bow in their natural shapes, but the only thing she was interested in liberating now was herself.

Inhaling a breath, she turned to Trent. "I'll be out of your hair by the time you get home from work."

"Work?" He frowned. "I'm not going in to work today."

Rebecca shrugged. "Regardless, I'll start moving my things right away."

"What the hell do you mean by that?" His voice was cool, each word given precision and weight. Even the curse word sounded calm, controlled.

"Trent." She lifted a hand, let it fall. "Our agreement is null and void, right? Because…well, because our baby is null and void." The phrase sounded ugly to her own ears, but she thought it was language that the CEO of Crosby Systems would understand.

His eyes narrowed. "So you're saying it's over. Everything we had."

"Everything we had is gone." She turned to walk up the stairs, aware he was following her. Rebecca wouldn't be able to pack to leave him if he was watching. "I don't need any help. I can do this by myself."

"Yeah, right," he muttered. "That's how you got both of us into this mess, isn't it? You thinking you could have a baby on your own."

Anger sparked inside her as she marched into the master bedroom and then to the closet. "And I could have done it by myself. That you were involved was something entirely unexpected. That you were Eisenhower's father was a—"

"Don't say mistake," he said flatly. "Don't you dare call it a mistake."

Rebecca rolled her eyes as she grabbed an armful of clothes off the closet pole. "Still unable to admit to anything human like one of those, Trent?" Realizing she didn't have a suitcase out, she crossed to the bed and dropped her load on the mattress.

"Don't do this, Rebecca."

She forced herself to look at him. "I'm sorry, Trent. You're right. You're a good man. I truly believe that. A good man and a conscientious one. But your responsibilities are over now."

"Rebecca…"

He had to let her go. He had to let her go while she was still dry-eyed. "We have nothing in common, Trent. Wasn't that clear to both of us? The CEO and the nurse. The woman who was used to home-cooked meals and the man accustomed to country-club business dinners. While I appreciate that your conscience won't let you kick me out—"

"Yes, I'm not kicking you out, let's get that very clear. For the record, apparently you're walking out."

And if he didn't look so contained, it might be harder. But his face was set in composed lines, as if they were discussing points on a contract instead of the rest of their lives. His rigid posture reminded her of those tortured flowers downstairs. "Let me go now, Trent. It will come to that, anyway."

"Are you so sure? What about—" He broke off, spun

around. With quick strides he took himself to the window and stared out.

Rebecca sank to the mattress. "What about what?"

"We were good together in bed. We were good with each other's friends. My family likes you."

Rebecca heard his mother's voice, from the country-club dance. *Marrying a Crosby is always a mistake.* "That's not enough for me, Trent."

"There is more, damn it." But despite the heated words, his voice was cool, his expression was cool as he turned to face her again. "I know there's more between us."

"Like what?" She was so tired. She wanted to go somewhere, curl up alone and try to heal her broken heart. Noticing that one of his dress shirts was on the top of her pile, she lifted it, meaning to put it aside. Instead, bowing her head, she crushed it against her. As protection? As comfort? "Like what, Trent? Name something. Name one thing more."

"Love."

Her gaze jerked up. Had he guessed? Did he know? Did he want her to stay because he felt sorry for her? As obligated now by her feelings as he had been when she was pregnant with his baby? Her fingers tightened on the crisp cotton shirt. "You don't believe in love."

"What if I told you different?" He made a short, vague gesture. "I've seen love around here. Felt it."

So he did know she was in love with him. And he was trying to mirror it back to her.

Oh, God, he was good. A good man for taking his

responsibilities so seriously. But he'd had other times, more appropriate times, to share his feelings with her, meaning this was just another of his business strategies—tell the opponent exactly what they want to hear. Not that he'd been able to put voice to the words, anyway.

"Trent, you don't look like a man who feels love. You look like a man who sets his mind on something and then sticks to it. But you can let it go now, Trent. You can let *me* go."

"Rebecca—"

"You can't go through the motions and call it love, Trent. I'm sorry, but you're too dispassionate a man ever to make me believe it."

And as if to prove her point, without another word her husband walked out of the room and out of the house and out of her life.

Without thinking, Trent drove to Crosby Systems and walked past Claudine's empty desk to retreat to his office. He shut the door behind him and put his mahogany desk between himself and the rest of the world.

This was his world, he thought, staring down at the piles of reports and pink slip messages stacked up on the surface. *This* would always be here to fill his time and give his life meaning.

Trent, you don't look like a man who feels love.

You can't go through the motions and call it love, Trent. I'm sorry, but you're too dispassionate a man ever to make me believe it.

The intercom buzzed. He pressed the answer button. "Yes?"

Claudine's voice lashed him. "What are you doing here?"

"I run the place." He flicked off the button.

Another buzz. Angry, like a bee intent on stinging. Latching tight his iron control, he answered again. "Yes?"

"What are you doing here today?"

What else was there to do? His wife was packing up to leave him, and he'd decided not to stick around and watch. Even if he had told her to stay because he loved her, she wouldn't have believed him. So what was the point?

"What are you doing here *today?*" Claudine demanded again.

"Working, you fishwife," he told Claudine through the intercom. "Work is what I do."

Since he'd said it, he'd have to follow through with it. He pulled closer to him the nearest file and opened the manila cover. Then slammed it shut. It was a file he'd borrowed from Katie—from Peter, really. His brother-in-law had done exhaustive research on the best strollers, crib mattresses and baby seats.

Trent had borrowed it. Now he couldn't bear having the damn thing in his office. Deciding to have Katie come retrieve it, he buzzed her office. No answer.

Fine. He stuffed the plump file at the bottom of the pile on his desk and picked up the next in the stack. But the one on the bottom continued to distract him. A slick magazine article was half sticking out, giving him a glimpse of a stuffed animal.

With a curse, he tried his sister's office again. Again, no answer. He tried her assistant. No answer.

He buzzed Claudine. "Where the hell is everybody?" he demanded.

Her sigh gusted through the speaker. "Who do you need, boss?"

Rebecca. Eisenhower. He needed his life as it had been shaping up to be. He shoved the thoughts from his head. "Where's my sister?" The file was glowing like uranium.

"At home."

"Home? Isn't she a vice president here? Doesn't she have something to do that is business-related?"

"She's working from home today, you tyrant. Perhaps you should do the same."

He scowled at the intercom. "You're fired. Work up the papers."

"Fine, I'll get right on it next week. Sooner, if you don't screw your head on straight, Trent. You have another place to be now. Other things to tend to."

"Rebecca wants to be alone." He couldn't admit she didn't want him. Not yet. "She's upset about the miscarriage."

"Aren't you?"

"Of course." Yes. But he wasn't going to think about it. How could another child be lost? No, no, no. His heart was expanding again, crowding out everything in his chest so his breath couldn't make it to his lungs.

Forget about the baby. Forget about everything but work.

His gaze caught on that infant paraphernalia file again. He had to get rid of the damned thing. "I have a short errand. You can reach me at Katie's."

A short drive later, his sister answered her door with words that echoed Claudine's. "What are you doing here?"

He shoved the file folder at her. "I brought you this." As he turned away, she grabbed his arm.

"Not so fast. I want to hear how Rebecca's doing. How *you're* doing."

"You don't need to worry about me. Rebecca's leaving."

"What?"

What it was, was that he'd been duped again, he decided. Before he'd met Rebecca, he'd been smart. He'd been aware that love was a myth that people like his sister and Peter told themselves to weave something spiritual into their sexual attraction. But then Rebecca had come along. All her softness had rubbed away the hard edges of his cynicism. He'd let himself get vulnerable again—to her, to feeling.

It had all gone to hell once he stopped expecting the worst of people, he realized. "Same song, second verse," he said to his sister.

"What?" Then her gaze darted over his shoulder. "We can't talk about this right at the moment. The police have just arrived."

Trent blinked, then glanced around. "The police?"

"My in-laws are inside and some detectives called not long ago, wanting to speak with them. To make a long story short, they're meeting here."

"I'll go—"

"No!" Katie's grip on his arm tightened. "I don't want you getting away from me until we've had a chance to talk this out."

Trent didn't know why he let her drag him into the house. Well, yeah, he did. He didn't want to be alone with his own company now. As Katie greeted the police officers, he poked his head into the living room to say hello to Peter and his parents. "I'll just hang out in your study, if that's okay," he said to his brother-in-law.

It was Mrs. Logan who answered, giving him another of her warm, wonderful smiles. "Trent, you're family, remember? And we're told this has something to do with Children's Connection. You already know what's been going on there, so sit down." She glanced at her husband. "Terrence agrees with me, right?"

Though Terrence didn't look as certain as his wife, he nodded. Trent figured the older couple had been married for close to forty years, and he wondered how they'd managed that. Respect, he decided. And trust. If love was a sham, a shallow, fickle feeling that described that sizzle of one woman's skin against one man's, then a long-term marriage must last due to respect and trust.

Or not. Because, hell, he'd respected Rebecca. As for trust…

You didn't trust her enough to tell her your feelings, a little voice whispered. *Not any of them.*

At that moment, Katie ushered the police detectives into the living room. After being introduced to Detective Levine, a middle-aged man, and a younger woman, Detective Ellen Slater, both from the Portland P.D., Trent retreated to an out-of-the-way corner.

"Mr. and Mrs. Logan, we have some news about your son Robbie."

Robbie! Trent found himself leaning forward in his distant seat.

"News about Robbie?" Leslie Logan repeated. "But I thought—"

"Twenty-eight years ago, did you know any persons by the name of Joleen and Lester Baker?"

The older Logans looked at each other, then shook their heads.

The detective twisted in his chair to pin Trent with his gaze. "What about you, Mr. Crosby? Do those names ring any bells?"

Thinking back, Trent repeated the names in his mind. "No. I was only nine, you understand, but I don't recognize them."

"What exactly are you saying?" Terrence asked calmly. He had reached over to clasp his wife's hand, but he looked at perfect peace. "Are those the people who stole our son?"

"Yes." The detective nodded. "What we've been able to piece together is that Lester Baker lured Robbie into his truck. Because of your wealth, the investigators at the time hoped to hear from the kidnapper about a ransom, but the truth is that Lester quickly drove out of town and to his wife, Joleen. They'd lost a child years before and Lester brought Robbie to her as a replacement for their son."

"Are they…a nice couple?" Leslie whispered.

Detective Levine grimaced. "From the information we've been able to gather, they're both gone now, but no, Mrs. Logan, I can't say they were a nice couple. They drank, they were known for running when the law or a landlord got too close. They hopscotched around Ohio, Michigan and Indiana. Ten years after the abduction, Lester left his wife and the boy and was later killed in a accident. Joleen lived until 2001, when she died of liver cancer."

"And my son?" Leslie's face had lost its color, but her voice was stronger than before.

"Right before Joleen Baker died, he discovered what had happened to him as a little boy."

"What do you mean?" Terrence asked. "He didn't remember?"

Detective Levine shook his head, then gestured to his partner.

"Mr. and Mrs. Logan," the woman began. "Besides being a detective for the Portland police, I'm a psychologist. I was asked to consult on this case. You need to understand that on the ride away from the Crosby house that November twenty-eight years ago, your son was given a sedative, and then more doses for several days thereafter. The drugs and the trauma were the first and very effective tools in brainwashing your Robbie. The human mind is elastic and resilient, and Robbie did what he had to do to survive." She paused, looking back and forth between the couple.

"Please go on," Terrence prompted.

"The Bakers told Robbie that he'd been bad. That his parents didn't want him any longer."

Leslie gasped. "Surely Robbie didn't believe that! He knew how much we loved him!"

Detective Slater nodded. "In some ways, that made it even more imperative that Robbie bury his old life and accept the new one. The love that he remembered hurt very, very much when he could see that returning to you was not within his power. So he came to accept this new identity as protection from the sometimes violent Bakers and as protection from the bittersweet memories of the past."

Leslie put one hand up to her mouth. Peter rushed to his mother's side. "Mom? Can I get you something?" He glanced over at his father whose composed expression hadn't cracked. "Dad, are you all right?"

"I'm fine, son." He inhaled a slow breath. "So then what happened?"

The psychologist-detective glanced at Leslie and hesitated.

Trent felt his hands fist. What had happened to little Robbie? There must be ice water in Terrence Logan's veins if he could sit there like that, as if he was etched out of stone.

"Robbie found out the truth from Joleen shortly before she died, after he had put himself through college and was working at a good job in St. Louis. He was stunned. Any memories that had ever bubbled up, he'd dismissed as fantasies."

"But 2001," Peter put in. "That was years ago. Why didn't he contact Mom and Dad?"

"He'd gone through a lot with the Bakers," Detective Slater started to say, then stopped. "More than a lot. In his mind, after what he'd experienced, he felt he wasn't good enough for your family."

"Not good enough?" Katie rose to stand behind her mother-in-law, putting her hands on the older woman's shoulders. "That doesn't make sense."

"Some part of him blamed himself. He thought that he was the one who should have managed to break free and find his way back to the family," the detective said.

Leslie sank back into the pillows of the couch. "My boy." Tears began rolling down her cheeks. "My poor boy."

Katie looked over at Trent. She was crying, too. And thinking what he was, Trent guessed. What if their nephew, Danny's Noah, was under the control of people like the Bakers? Peter glanced at his wife, saw her distress and rose hurriedly to take her into his arms.

Trent's fists tightened and he wondered why it was so damn cold in his corner. Katie and Peter had a drafty house.

"Mr. and Mrs. Logan," Detective Levine took over the story now. "I don't know how to tell you this—"

"Straight out," Terrence Logan said. "Just give it to us straight out."

The detective nodded. "Your son moved to the Portland area, but he couldn't bring himself to contact you. He got mixed up with some bad people, Mr. and Mrs. Logan. Some very bad people."

Terrence nodded slowly. "You're telling me that Robbie isn't dead."

"You're right. Robbie is in our custody and he's pleaded guilty to a variety of crimes committed under the name Everett Baker."

"Everett Baker?" Leslie echoed, sounding stunned.

Everett Baker! Trent *was* stunned. When the police had quizzed them about a Lester and Joleen Baker, Trent, for one, hadn't put the last names together.

My God, my God. Robbie Logan was Everett Baker.

"Everett Baker?" Terrence said it, too. It was impossible to know what he was thinking, his face was expressionless, his voice neutral.

Ice water in his veins, Trent thought again. And a refrigerator compressor for a heart. Rebecca accused *him* of being emotionless, but Terrence Logan was the real robot of Portland.

But this is just how you appear to Rebecca, that little voice said.

Leslie gazed at her husband, then looked up at Peter and Katie. "He's alive!" And then she slumped over.

Everyone rushed to her side, and it only took a second or two to rouse her again. Katie and Peter wanted to call an ambulance, but Leslie assured them she was fine. "The excitement," she said. They'd bundled her in a blanket, and above the thick fabric, her face had new color. There was a new brightness in her eyes. She held out her hand to Terrence. "Darling, our Robbie! Our Robbie!"

He brought his wife's hand to his mouth and smiled. It was the first real emotion that Trent had seen the man reveal.

And then Terrence wept, still wearing that smile on his face.

Astounded by the change in the older man, Trent took an instinctive step back. His shoulder hit Peter's and he looked over at his brother-in-law. "Your father…" He gestured at the man who was holding on to his wife and crying those silent, smiling tears. "Is your father all right?"

Peter nodded. "Dad holds on to his cool with a stronger grip than any other man I know. But don't make the mistake of thinking him heartless."

Don't make the mistake of thinking him heartless. One look at Terrence sharing his emotion with his wife and there was no doubt he was anything but.

Terrence looked up, his gaze taking in Peter and Trent. "Our child is alive!"

And Trent thought he understood a tiny measure of the other man's joy, because Trent's child was not.

Before he could let that thought overtake him, before he started screaming with the pain of leaking emotion, he rushed away from Katie's house.

Fifteen

Rebecca heard the front door of Trent's house slam shut and poked her head out of the den. He stood in the foyer. Somewhere since she'd last seen him, he'd shed his sport coat and tie. His hair was rumpled and the cuffs of his dress shirt were rolled up unevenly. She'd never seen him appear so disordered. "You're back," she said.

He looked at her, then looked around him. "I suppose I am," he said, as if he was mildly surprised to find himself there.

"Well, good."

He looked even more surprised at that. "Good?"

"I could use some help." She kept her voice brisk. "Come into the den."

By the time he made it into the other room, she had blinked away the pinpricks at the corners of her eyes.

"What is it you need?" he asked.

You. Us. Everything the way it was, only better. But that could never be, so she pushed it out of her head. "The playhouse is too big to fit through the den door. Maybe between the two of us we could squash it a little or slant it or something."

He shoved his hands in his pockets and tilted his head as if considering the idea. She looked back at the playhouse herself. There was little else to do before it was ready for Merry. Over the past week, they'd finished the construction and then she'd put down tarps on her day off and painted the palace a bright green, with purple "bricks" around the door and windows. The roof was blue, the drawbridge as well. Multicolored daisies "grew" out of the grass lining the bottom of the walls.

Rebecca bent to lift the drawbridge. She pushed it over the door opening and felt the Velcro fasteners—Trent's brilliant idea—latch it closed. Then she scooted around the backside and gave it a little shove that moved it forward a couple of inches. "Or maybe if I pushed and you pulled…"

Trent pulled, and it slid toward the entry a few feet. "It's too big," he called out. "We're never going to manage it this way."

"But I have to take it with me!" She couldn't leave anything of herself behind. She just couldn't. "There must be a way."

There was another moment of silence. Then she heard Trent's footsteps in the kitchen. She heard him open a drawer, then close it. "You can use this," he said.

Rebecca came around the side to face him again. In his hand, he carried a tool. He held it out to her, his palm up.

She stared at what he offered. A box cutter. Swallowing hard, she lifted her gaze to his. "You expect me to cut apart Merry's castle?"

"You want it out of here, then that's what it takes."

Her hand reached for the tool. Her fingers hovered over it.

With a breath, she forced them lower.

He closed his own fingers over the cutter, dropped his arm to his side. "Don't do this, Rebecca," he said. "Don't destroy something we built together."

"But there isn't another way," she whispered. "You said it yourself."

His mouth compressed to a thin line. "It could stay right where it is. *You* could stay right where you are."

"Trent—"

"It's stuck here, Rebecca. Just like you're stuck in my heart."

She shook her head so hard that tendrils flew free of her ponytail. "No. No. You don't want me. You don't want that."

"Well, hell, Rebecca, maybe I'm not glad about it," he said, his tone impatient. "Maybe I was accustomed to spending eighteen hours a day in my office. Maybe I was *good* at being Trent Crosby, workaholic CEO, when I'm obviously lousy at being Trent Crosby, Rebecca's husband and lover. But it's not as if I have any choice."

"It's that you feel responsible for me."

He sighed. "You give me way too much credit."

She didn't think so. This was the man who'd practically raised his brother and sisters. The man who'd been nine years old when he'd felt guilty about another child being abducted from his home.

"Then it's that our marriage was a mistake you don't want to admit to," she said, throwing everything she could think of at him in order to keep herself safe.

His jaw set and he took a step closer to her. "I'm admitting I was wrong about love, aren't I? Because that's what I'm saying, Rebecca. I'm saying I love you. I'm saying I'm in love with you."

"No." One part of her wanted to turn ballerina and go up on tiptoes, there to twirl and swirl to music that was swelling in her head. But she couldn't allow herself to believe that. "No."

"Damn it!" It wasn't exactly yelling, but it was the loudest voice she'd ever heard him use. He tossed the box cutter into a corner. "What does it take to get through to you, Rebecca?"

Tears gushed from her eyes and washed down her cheeks. He'd gotten to her already. Days ago. Weeks ago. But she couldn't let him know, so she swiped at the wetness on her cheeks. "I'm sorry, I'm sorry. It's the hormones. The doctor said my emotions might roller-coaster like this."

"Oh, hell, Rebecca." He reached out and pulled her into his arms. "Don't you see that now is not the right time to make a decision like this?"

She wanted to move away from him. She really did. Instead she stood in the warm circle of his arms, shaking her head.

"You're not yourself."

More wetness soaked into his starchy dress shirt, then she lifted her head to meet his gaze. "This *is* me," she said. "This is me, Trent. I'm afraid. You didn't believe in love. I didn't believe it could ever happen to me. This thing between us must be something else. It *must* be."

With his hands still on her shoulders, he backed off a little more to look into her face. "I don't know the counter answer to that. I don't know what changed. We found ourselves in a situation—"

"By mistake."

He put his hand over her mouth. "We found ourselves in a situation that gave us a chance to find each other. And what did we do then?"

"We talked ourselves into getting married and then we made a mess of it."

"We made this castle, Rebecca. We built something that reflected what was building inside of us."

She snatched his hand away from her mouth. "I have to point out that *you* were the one who appointed yourself royal architect."

"I did, didn't I? Does that mean I get the credit for believing in our happy ending first?"

Rebecca stepped away, her hand going to her abdomen. "There wasn't a happy ending."

He sucked in a breath. "Not the one we were planning, maybe. But think about this. If Eisenhower had been born, we would have always considered we *had* to get married. This way we know we *chose* to be together."

"You're trying to use logic on me again, aren't you?"

His half smile was rueful. "I don't suppose that means it's working?"

She couldn't deny him any longer. What was the point? "All right, Trent. All right. I do love you. I am in love with you." Her hand came up as he moved toward her. "But I—I need something more from you. There's still something missing."

"What?" he demanded. "What could possibly be missing?"

He *talked* about what was in his heart, but she hadn't seen it. She shrugged.

Gazing at her, he shook his head. "You're a tough sell, Rebecca Crosby, do you know that?"

"I'm not one of your clients, Trent." That was it, she realized. Though he'd managed to say the words straight out, she was afraid he was still figuring the angles, still working the business meeting, going down points on some prepared agenda.

That impatient note entered his voice again. "I came back today because I believe in you. In us. What does a man have to do to prove that to you, Rebecca?"

"Show me your heart, Trent." She didn't know how to explain it any plainer than that. "Don't talk about what's there. *Show* me."

He ran his hands through his hair. "I drink your green tea—"

"Show me."

"Damn it! Last Sunday I folded laun—"

"Show me."

He stared at her, frustration, exasperation apparent in his tousled hair and fuming expression. At least he looked a little less perfect than usual. "Damn it, Rebecca," he repeated. Then, bowing his head, he murmured something strange. "This is all your fault, Terrence Logan."

Then Trent jerked up his head and caught Rebecca's gaze. His hands lifted and he yanked the edges of his dress shirt apart. Buttons pinged against the cardboard castle.

She blinked. "What...?" And then she saw it. On a longer chain than the one he'd given her. But she recognized the tiny figure. The Eisenhower angel, dangling right in the middle of Trent's chest.

"You left it on the bathroom sink," he said, his voice hoarse. "The night you were in the hospital, I picked it up and...and I couldn't put it down again."

Her gaze rose to his face and what she saw there paralyzed her. Gone was the cool, composed Trent she'd marveled at a thousand times. In his place was a warm-blooded man who felt sadness, anguish, grief. A man who really, truly *felt*.

His hand covered his heart and then he turned away from her. "Oh, God, Rebecca. God, Rebecca, we lost Eisenhower."

She melted. Her frozen muscles as well as her formidable fears. She flew to him. Her arms about him, she pressed her cheek against his back. This man who hadn't wanted to lose another child. "I know, Trent. I know, my love."

Then she pulled him down to the ugly black couch with her and held him tight. He rested his head against the top of hers and then moved it down to kiss her cheek. It was wet; she must be crying again. No, it was Trent. Rocking back and forth, they comforted each other with words she would never remember.

The words didn't matter. Their hearts did. Broken, healed, broken again. Then healed for good.

Trent pulled away to cup her face in his hands and brush her tears away with his thumbs. "I'm sorry. I'm so sorry. I was afraid that facing the truth would make the pain more real. But it hurts either way. I'm so sad that we lost our baby."

But found each other.

Rebecca placed her hand against the Eisenhower angel over Trent's heart. Their other angel was up there somewhere, right? Smiling? Waiting for a different moment to enter their lives?

Of course that was it.

"I love you," Trent said.

And this time she felt it, saw it, knew it.

Rebecca looked over at the castle, then gazed back on her husband. With Trent right by her side, she had that someone of her own to love she'd wanted all her life. Together, it was going to be all right. Together, it wasn't so hard to believe in happy endings anymore.

* * * * *

after
The
heated,
fire
brush
so se
the

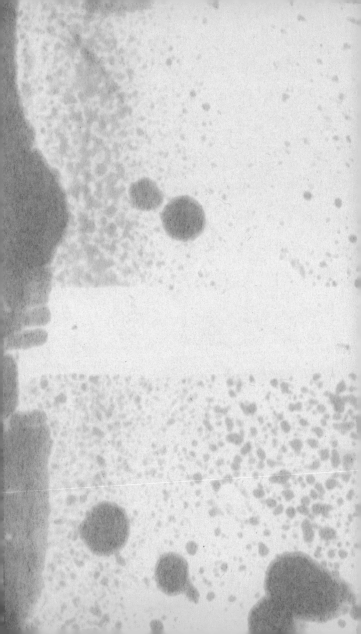